PRAISE FOR A. R. SILVERBERRY

Praise for The Stream

"**Wend's story is heart-breaking,** joyous, desperate and exciting . . . Masterful storytelling and a thought-provoking read." Five Stars! Readers' Favorite Review

"**This book is nothing less than a treasure!**" Janetti Marotta, PhD, author of 50 Mindful Steps to Self-Esteem: Everyday Practices for Cultivating Self-Acceptance & Self-Compassion

Praise for Wyndano's Cloak

"**Constant suspense . . . impossible to put down**. You're going to be very tired in the morning!" Feathered Quill Review

"**I was entranced** . . . Silverberry is a master at characterization. Few are his equal . . ." Readers Favorite

"**I loved it!** If you like a tight, well-written, exciting, moving, and, ultimately, satisfying book, then this is for you, regardless of your age and gender." The Book Sage, Review by Lloyd Russell

"**A tale of intense imagination and wonder**. An adventure we may only find in the deepest corners of our imagination. A. R. Silverberry's story was one that I will likely be re-reading very soon." Allbooksreviews, Review by Kirsten Bussière

"**A grand adventure . . . a coming-of-age soon to be classic.** Silverberry's creativity and imagination are second to none." Review by William R. Potter for Reader's Choice Book Reviews

"**An extraordinary heroine** . . . captures the courage and sense of adventure that lies in the heart of all young girls." Sandra Martz, editor, *When I Am an Old Woman I Shall Wear Purple*

"**Mystery, treachery, intrigue** . . . and a magical cloak that may prove just as dangerous to use as not to use. Delicious!" Eric A. Kimmel, author of *Hershel and the Hanukkah Goblins*

"**A magical tale** . . . chock full of everything a great fantasy novel needs; dashing young men, adventures galore, treachery, love and intrigue ... I highly recommend this book." Thesupermom.com, Review by Karlynn Johnston

"**Hard to put down!!!** Breathtaking and Captivating tale of a brave and daring young girl!" Marcia Freespirit, CEO, JimSam Publishing

CERBERUS

TALES OF MAGIC AND MALICE

A. R. SILVERBERRY

TREE TUNNEL PRESS

Cover Design © SelfPubBookCovers.com/ Viergacht

Print Edition ISBN - 13: 978-0-9841037-9-9
Print Edition ISBN - 10: 0-9841037-9-1

Published by Tree Tunnel Press, P.O. Box 733, Capitola, CA 95010

First Edition. Printed in the United States of America
0987654321

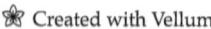 Created with Vellum

To Sherry,

For bringing the magic

CONTENTS

PREVIEW OF WYNDANO'S CLOAK

PREFACE

Though he penned some of the most memorable novels in science fiction, Ray Bradbury thought of himself as a sprinter, a short story writer. I always thought of myself as a marathoner. Blame my personality. Big things done alone have always appealed to me. In elementary school, I challenged the "fastest kid in the class" to an endurance race around the schoolyard. By lap nineteen he dropped out clutching his side. I kept going another ten laps, even though I was running solo. When I discovered novel writing, it seemed just the thing. The form allows for the creation of intricate worlds, twisty plots, and complex and compelling characters. And plenty of time for the story to unfold. It came as a surprise, then, that I would enjoy writing short stories. The concentration of time, place, and emotions was startling and satisfying. And there's nothing like knocking out a finished piece in a few days or weeks, rather than one to three years, my pace for writing a novel.

In this volume, three stories sprouted from prompts from The Fellowship of Fantasy, an online support group for fantasy authors. One of these stories, "Three Steaks and a Box of Chocolates," was published in their anthology, *Fantastic*

Creatures. Another, "The Demon Monkeys," was published in their anthology *Hall of Heroes.* "Blaze" was also inspired by the story prompt for *Fantastic Creatures,* but you can't always control when something is ready, and it needed more time to gel. "Cerberus" on the other hand had been rolling around my brain for some time. The prompt for that first anthology fit it to a tee, but I decided to retain it for later publication. Two unfinished stories, "The Tea Party" and "The Mask," were dredged out of old computer files and completed for this collection.

Flash fiction lends itself wonderfully to fairy tales, and I couldn't resist conjuring up two of these with "The Willow Princess" and "Tangles." A third flash fiction, "Titania," was inspired by the magical forest in Shakespeare's *A Midsummer Night's Dream.*

So there you have it: mix six short stories with three flash fiction stories and you get a potion for magic and malice. I hope you enjoy reading these as much as I did writing them.

INTRODUCTION

Mystery and magic reside in both strange and mundane places. The same may be said of the heroes and heroines, big or small, who quest there as well as the beasts, human or otherwise, that they battle. Skeptical? Take a gander at the locales and folk that occupy the tales in this volume.

Three Steaks and a Box of Chocolates: Stuck in a desolate town and down on his luck, Doc Turner takes on a mysterious case. He gets more than he bargained for.

Cerberus: Bailiff Giles Dunstable is hell-bent on stopping the spread of superstition in his village. But his beliefs are sorely tested after the witch of the Hevyl Mountains reads his fortune.

The Willow Princess: Separated in childhood, two sisters struggle against a terrible enchantment to reunite and claim their birthright.

The Demon Monkeys: The mountain hides a secret. Deep in winter, the orphan girl Scamp fights to survive in the shadow of a menacing terror. When a stranger crosses her path, her life changes forever.

Tangles: Lessy needs one last spell. But it, like everything else, has faded.

Titania: After a mysterious encounter on her doorstep, a reclusive actress battles doubt and disability to take on her greatest role.

Blaze: In 1689, the lonely servant boy Davie fights to protect his one friend from the malice of a heartless earl.

The Tea Party: A dying Sir Robert Wainwright offers his selfish sons one last invitation to tea …

The Mask: Jessica Lansing is certain her tyrannical methods will win her Teacher of the Year. But her plans start to unravel when little Christopher makes a singular mask.

This 'twas but a sip, dear reader. For the full spell, drink on …

THREE STEAKS AND A BOX OF CHOCOLATES

The day Burt McCall backfired into Dead End I got my last and most peculiar patient. I'd been standing on the termite-riddled planks of the sidewalk watching dust devils and my sign swinging in the wind. The two customers in the Dry Gulch Saloon hadn't moved in their chairs all day. For all anyone knew, they could've been dead.

Then Burt parked in front of the post office and that got my attention. If he had anyone to write to, no one knew about it. He came out a minute later with a small package. He tossed it into his tow truck and headed across the street to my establishment.

"Why don't you take that rusty can of yours out of town before you hurt someone?" I said, itching to know what was in the package.

"I ain't happy to see you, either," he replied. "But I got something that needs doctorin'."

I looked him over. From his worn boots to his weathered face, he was none too pretty to look at. But a wealth of silver tumbled from beneath his old hat, and his eyes hadn't lost their youthful spark.

"You never paid for last time," I said.

"I'd think you'd want the business." He stared meaning-fully at my sign:

DOC TURNER
HEALING ARTIST

Its groaning in the wind seemed to emphasize his point. Fact was, no one had passed beneath it for quite a spell. I admit I'd tightened my belt a notch or three.

"This better be good," I said.

Inside my office, he reached into his pocket, pulled out a lump of gold, and slammed it on my desk. "That oughtta cover what I owe. Consider the rest a down payment. You'll get a whole lot more if you help me."

"Is it real?"

"Test it yourself."

I didn't need to. I'd seen enough nuggets to know the real McCoy from the metal of fools—though, as for fools, Burt might take the cake. He seemed to make a profession of chasing crackpot dreams.

"You didn't pull this from that sand patch of yours. Who'd you steal it from? That way, I'm prepared when they come after me for it."

"Now that plain hurts, Doc. I've been tellin' you all along there's gold there, and there's the proof. Just like I told you there's water."

"The day you find water I eat my boots."

"Then you better put a fire under the pot so you can cook 'em when you get back. You gonna help me or not?"

I rose, put on my hat, and grabbed my medicine bag. Business had dried up since the new doctor set up down in Black Rock. He was young and knew how to charm the ladies. I'm past my prime on that score and maybe behind the times in doctoring. I figured Burt's gold would cover me for six months. Mainly, I wanted something to do besides watching dust devils. If anything else was happening in Dead End, nobody told me about it.

"Well, what do you need me for?" I asked.

"Fluffy ain't feelin' good."

"You want me to drive all the way over to your dump in this heat for a cat? Anyway, you don't like cats."

He gave me a sly smile. "I don't. Fluffy's special."

I let that slide. "What's wrong with her?"

"I think she's got a toothache." He was looking at a photo on my wall, me standing beside a sleeping elephant, a red-and-white big top in the background. "You sure you didn't kill that elephant?"

"Couldn't. He was the circus's prize possession. But he went berserk when they sold his lady friend. Elephants are loyal that way. I used something that would drop a dinosaur and they paid me well for it." I was feeling a little sad thinking about it. It was probably the last good bit of coin I'd seen. If things didn't turn around soon, I'd have to close shop. The thought of moving at my age didn't appeal to my bones, which were about as shaky as Burt's truck.

"You still got that tranquilizer?"

"Probably somewhere."

"Get it. Fluffy doesn't like pain."

I squinted at him like he was a crazy man, which he probably was. That didn't matter. He wouldn't drive clear to Dead End unless he needed to. Something was afoot, and I aimed to find out what. I threw some hypos and elephant tranquilizer into my bag. We piled into his truck and started bouncing down the road, sending up clouds of dust.

I hung on for fear of falling out. "If you'd brush that cat's teeth, it wouldn't have a toothache."

"I never heard of such a thing." He grinned with those yellow teeth of his.

"Tackling your own once a week might not be a bad idea either."

He came to a sudden stop in front of Newsom's Hardware. "Fine."

He hopped out and a minute later returned with a push broom and a crowbar.

"What's that for?"

"An ounce of prevention."

How many times the engine exploded no one would want to find out, but an hour later his mountain came into view. As the story goes, a bespectacled gent named Norman Fable from one of those big universities back east inspected it for a mining company. He declared it a likely place to find gold or silver. Everyone and their uncle descended on the place. For two decades they punched holes all over it and found zip. Now most people call it Fable Mountain. It seems a respectable way to immortalize the man.

The Indians round here call it Awanyu, after their serpent god. They got it right. From this side, it looked like a snake stretched out on the desert floor, the east peak its head, the west peak an eroded cliff that curved up like a tail.

Miles passed with nothing but cactuses, the sweat on the back of your neck, and horse flies the size of buffaloes. Burt was by himself out here. A lonely feeling settled into my bones.

His lean-to came into view, stuck against the base of the mountain. There wasn't a well in sight.

"How do you survive out here without water?"

He gave me that sidelong look again. "I got water."

"You old fibber. The only water is floating around your brain."

"Well, you can add your hat to your boots. Looks like you're losin' weight, anyway."

"I mean it, Burt. How do you get by?" Fact was, I cared about him.

He pointed to a clay disk with painted triangles and spirals hanging from his rearview mirror. "Amulets."

"You can't get by on luck."

"It ain't luck. It's magic. That's what Indian Bob says. He oughtta know."

"If that's from Indian Bob you got swindled. He's no more Indian than you are."

"Not so, I'm two-thirds Hopi and two-thirds Chippewa."

"Where do the McCalls fit in?"

"The lost tribe. You can't count 'em."

I didn't want to argue. He was rather sensitive on the subject, and told all kinds of tales about giant bears, birds, and skunks, and rolling heads that gobbled up bad people. He swore he'd seen them hereabouts, but then again, he'd claimed he'd seen a sea serpent in his navy days. Said it would bring him luck one day.

He pulled up to the lean-to and took up his package and the broom and crowbar he'd bought at Newsom's. I followed him inside, hoping it would be cooler. The concept of shade didn't seem to apply there, and sweat was rolling down my face. He offered me a pull from a canteen. I expected the water to be dusty. It was surprisingly cold and sweet.

He watched me drink. "Don't be bashful. There's plenty where that came from."

I didn't need a second invitation and poured half of it down my shirt. When the last drop trickled down my throat, I looked at him guiltily. "Sorry, I should've left you some."

He shrugged. "Take it, we'll refill it."

I looked around, trying to figure this out. No well outside. Not even a water tank. An old wood-burning stove sat in one corner, a narrow cot in the other. An iron skillet, a Dutch oven, and a big spoon hung from the ceiling. A buffalo hide was nailed to one wall, probably to cover gaps in the planks that bands of light would've streamed through. More amulets were scattered about, long feathers, beads, bits of carved turquoise, dreamcatchers. If he was finding his dreams, I couldn't see it.

The front of the room was as clean as any bachelor's, but toward the rear, a layer of dirt covered the floor. A curtain hung over the back wall. It stirred, though no wind came through the open windows.

He lit a lantern and gave it to me. Smiling to himself, he put the package in a knapsack, slung it over his shoulder, and took up the broom and crowbar.

With my medicine bag in one hand and the lantern in the other, I followed him to the curtain, wondering what all this was leading to. He parted the curtain. More dirt was piled to the left and right but dead ahead the wall had been torn away, revealing an opening large enough to step through.

Inside, the temperature dropped. At first, I thought this was a mineshaft from the Fable days, but the walls were rocky and irregular, suggesting it was a cave. I turned to look back at the dirt piled near the opening. It looked fresh.

"How'd you know to dig here?" I asked.

"I did a sweat with Indian Bob and had a vision. It showed me the spot."

The passage angled down. Cool air wafted from below. As pleasant as it was to get out of the heat, that forlorn feeling settled on me hard.

"Why do you live like this, Burt?"

His eyes were flames in the glow of the lantern. "Like what?"

"Alone. This place makes Dead End seem crowded."

"I'm not alone. I got Fluffy."

That didn't reassure me.

Neither of us spoke for a spell. He probably figured I'd run the other way if he said more. All I could do was see how this played out.

Finally he said, "If you found somethin' valuable, would you share it?"

I considered. If I wanted to be a Rockefeller, I'd have taken a different road. "Sure would. Guess I don't need much."

"That's what I figured. And we're friends, right? I can trust you?"

"I'd have to be to go along with whatever you're brewing here."

"Figured that too. That's why I came to you and not that fake in Black Rock." He wiped his eyes, which had grown misty. "Friendship's a rare thing, Doc." After a pause, he added, "Love, too."

A few steps farther the passage opened into a cavern so vast, the lantern couldn't penetrate the limits of it. What got my heart pounding was the low, rhythmic lapping of waves.

"Well, I'll be," I said. "You found water." And not just a trickle. This was a sea, broad, wide, and gleaming dimly.

Not far away, a deep moan echoed off the walls. I could conjure a lot of things in my mind and nothing to fit that sound. My heart froze.

I swallowed, trying to moisten my throat, which was drier than the Mojave. "Is that what you brought me here for?"

Burt set down the broom and crowbar and walked to the shore. "Yep."

"What is it?"

"You can decide for yourself."

I looked behind me, wondering how long it would take to get back to sunshine, where scorpions and hungry coyotes seemed suddenly friendly. "Maybe I don't want any part of it."

He turned back to me, hands on his hips. "You took a hippocritic oath."

"I'm beginning to feel like I did. Did I ever tell you I dropped out of medical school? Why do you think I opened shop in Dead End?"

He came up and put a reassuring hand on my shoulder. "That don't matter," he replied. "You can cure the warts off a hog. I'm livin' proof."

Small splashes drew near. Something was coming, cutting smoothly in and out of the water.

"Look, Doc, you don't have anythin' to worry about. I told you, she's a pussycat."

A groan like a sick cow reverberated through the chamber.

"Is that her meow?"

Burt wrung his hands. "She's in pain. I don't know what to do for her."

I waited, holding my breath, listening with dread and fascination as the splashes came on. Then I saw her, emerging from the darkness, first her eyes, shining like coins for a titan, then her brontosaurus head, which seemed to float above the water. A monstrous neck followed. Trailing thirty feet behind, her body looped through the water like a giant hose.

The water must have been deep almost up to the shore. She left her body submerged and dropped her head on a flat rock as a dog that was feeling pathetic and under the weather might.

Burt patted her head and scratched where her ears would be if she were a cat. "This here's the doctor I told you 'bout."

She moaned again, but not so loud. Her eyes rolled until they locked on me. They were intelligent and hopeful.

Since she hadn't snatched Burt in those jaws of hers and dragged him underwater, I approached.

"Why do you think it's her tooth?" I asked.

"She isn't eatin' normal."

"How do you know?"

"She won't touch anythin' I give her."

"What do you give her, a cow?"

He nodded to the water. "She catches lots of fish there. Three times a week I give her steak and some of these." He pulled the post-office package from his knapsack and unwrapped it. Inside was a box of Dormel's chocolates.

"You give her that?"

He gave me a bashful look. "She loves 'em."

I shook my head, pretty certain what the problem was. "Well, I better have a look. Will she open up and not snap my head off?"

He stroked her nose. "Let Doc have a look and I'll give you some of the toffee ones."

I swear she almost smiled at that and her head went up and down in what might have been a nod. She opened wide and displayed a set of nine-inch teeth the like of which haven't been seen since this planet's infancy.

I handed Burt the lantern. "If I die, I'll kill you."

He held it close while I bent in for a look. Those daggers were pearly white near the top, but a brown deposit had formed on the bottom. One back tooth looked pretty bad. The gum around it was swollen too.

I rose and tapped the chocolate box. "That's your problem. It'll rot her teeth in no time."

"Can you do somethin' for her?"

"A tooth has to come out." I rubbed my chin, studying her, trying to figure how to do it. She looked at me, her eyes innocent and trusting. If I hurt her she'd flail and make hamburger out of me with a whip from her tail, though she didn't mean a lick of harm.

"Thought so. Well, you brought the tranquilizer."

"That's not it, Burt. I can't exactly dig it out."

"You gotta help me, Doc. I'm lost without her."

He wasn't the only one. It dawned on me I'd been lost a long time. Maybe she was the way out. A strange urgency gripped me. I had to do this or I was a goner; I'd blow away like dust.

I looked around and then back the way we came. "How far is it to your cabin?"

"Maybe a hundred fifty feet."

"How much cable you got on your tow?"

His face lit up. "Two hundred."

"Let's prep her. I want her down deep when we do this."

9

Burt coaxed her mouth back open. "This is goin' to hurt a little. You just hold on. Doc's goin' to fix you up."

It might seem questionable to a sane person why I would put my faith in such reassurances, but I'd seen enough of her to risk it. I keep a supply of anesthetic in my bag and started with that, giving her a dozen shots around the tooth. For good measure, I added a few injections of penicillin. Next, I loaded four hypos with elephant tranquilizer. I didn't bring a gun and wouldn't have used it if I had. The sound would have scared her. I felt the scales on her throat and found a vein pulsing like a drum. Holding my breath, I stuck one in. She didn't flinch. Probably wasn't much more than a fleabite to her.

"Let's head up," I said, closing my bag. "Tell her to stay put. If she goes unconscious and slips into the water, she could drown."

"No sayin' what she'll do on drugs." He handed me the keys to his truck. "You get the cable. I'll keep an eye on her."

He had a point about the drugs. I thought I'd better stay in case she had a reaction. What I would do for a creature like her was up for question. They didn't cover that in medical school.

I glanced at my watch. "Tell you what, let's see how she does."

We waited fifteen minutes. Those giant eyes never closed. They did sink to half-mast. That great head of hers lolled on the rock.

"Let's go," I said. "We got about forty minutes to do this."

He squatted before her. "Don't go nowhere and I'll give you more of these." He held up the chocolates.

The dreamy expression on her face got dreamier.

We debated what she was on the way to his truck. Burt thought she was like that creature spotted in '33 in northern Scotland. Wherever she came from, I was pretty certain she was Awanyu. Stories come from somewhere. If you came right down to it, the Hopis got things right. Maybe Indian Bob had some of their blood after all.

To tell the truth, I was preoccupied with something else. How in the devil was I going to grab on to that tooth? I kept picturing it from all kinds of angles. The tooth broke in each scenario, leaving the root.

By the time we were topside, I thought of something. "Have you got a hand drill with a big bit?"

He found one in the back. The bit was just under an inch. It would have to do.

Burt backed his truck as close to the front door as he could. Using the hydraulic, he fed out both lines, which had swivel hooks attached to chains. He took one. I took the other. On the way back down, I studied the passage walls. I saw no evidence of prospecting. Where had he gotten that nugget?

When I asked, he gave me that sly smile. "Get that tooth out and you'll see."

Below, the creature still lolled at the water's edge. Her eyes hadn't closed, but the dreamy expression hadn't worn off, which gave me small comfort. I didn't know how she would react to what I had in mind or if it would even work.

Burt got her mouth open again. The tooth was conical. Using the drill at the base, I worked away at it, first on one side, then the other, enlarging both holes a little at a time. In my wildest dreams, I never thought I'd have my head so close to a monster's epiglottis. She was a good girl though and didn't stir once. Pretty soon the holes were large enough to work the hooks in.

Now came the tricky part. One of us had to go topside and retract the cable. She needed Burt to keep her calm, but she might need me for another shot. We flipped for it.

He went. I stayed.

"Stay put," he told her before leaving. "No matter what happens, stay put."

I watched the cable. We'd left some slack, so I'd have some

warning. I checked my watch every few minutes. The tranquilizer could wear off anytime. Bless his heart, it didn't take as long as I'd thought. I'm certain he ran all the way—he cared that much about her.

The cable pulled taut. Her eyes flared. With a cry she yanked her head back and out popped the tooth, as neat as a cork. I'm here to tell you it's hard to gauge a monster's expression, but this one seemed relieved.

I thought she might sink back to the rock. Instead, she reared back and dove, her long body flowing into the water.

Burt ran up, panting.

"Sorry," I said. "She's gone."

"She dove?"

I nodded.

He picked up the tooth and turned it in both hands. "She ain't gone. She's gettin' your reward."

Sure enough, she resurfaced and swam toward us with something gleaming in her mouth. When she reached the shore, she deposited a nugget the size of Kansas. Nearly a foot long, to be more precise.

Since then, I've debated with myself about what she was and whether others like her roam the rivers and byways underground. Sometimes I question if the whole thing happened, but the gold fetched a pretty penny, and I'm set up well now. I sold my practice in Dead End to a traveling snake oil salesman and moved to San Francisco, where the fog and ladies are more to my liking. Whatever happens from here on out, I won't end up beside those two hombres in the Dry Gulch Saloon.

Burt probably has more gold tucked away than me, but he stayed at the knees of Awanyu. I thought with all that water down there he'd license the rights or put in a golf course or something. He steadfastly refuses. To the world, he's a hermit. I know better. He found his life companion, and that's all there is to it.

Every now and then I get a letter from him. He tells me he brushes Fluffy's teeth regularly with the push broom and scores around her gumline with the crowbar. He doesn't live extravagantly, but pays for weekly deliveries.

I have it on high authority they consist of three steaks and a box of chocolates.

CERBERUS

*E*arly one morning, Charna Diyna, known as the witch of the Hevyl Mountains, set up her table in the marketplace of Wyebury village. She spread out a bright yellow cloth and began arranging amulets, ointments, potions, and herbs in rows according to categories. She had cures for sleep, cures for the gout, cures if you were too fat, cures if you were too thin, potions for getting into love, and potions for getting out. For special circumstances she had a few tricks up her sleeve, though no one sought these.

When the table was to her satisfaction, she took out a deck of prophecy cards, leaned back in her chair, and shuffled them while waiting for the first customers to arrive.

Word spread fast. They came, hurrying past cobbler tents and fabric stalls, forgoing the large baskets of apples, pears, and fish to catch sight of her. They formed a ring at a respectable distance, allowing others to go by and themselves a good look at her table. There were housewives, midwives, lords, ladies, peasants, peddlers, and troubadours. The butcher stepped from his stall to join them. Everyone chattered, arguing about what would happen when the bailiff got wind that she was here, and children skipped and cartwheeled in the dust and made small wagers about the outcome.

Charna Diyna proffered her cards to any who might want a reading. No one took her up on it. They were here for entertainment. When that passed, perhaps they would see what the future held for them. With a shrug of her humped shoulders, she poured a cup of cold buttermilk from a jug, leaned back in her chair, and sipped.

The crowd didn't have long to wait. Bailiff Giles Dunstable trod through the marketplace like a lord, his beetle-black brows knit, his enormous belly leading the way. He looked neither left nor right, but thrust his head forward like a hound sniffing a trail. When he reached the fishmonger's stall, he shouldered past the crowd and marched up to Charna's table.

"Hag," he said, "I promised to skin you if you returned."

She waved a gnarled hand over her wares. "You see I have nothing but herbs and spices."

"They're illegal."

A magpie landed on the striped awning above her and squawked, the sound like sharp laughter.

"I got most of them here last week," she said, waving toward the surrounding countryside. "When someone is sick, where would you have them go?"

"It's deviltry and witchcraft." He waved his fingers as if he were shooing a bug. "Move along, or you'll be thrown in the stockade."

She folded her arms. "What's the complaint? I relieve pain, I offer hope."

He pointed to her cards. "You corrupt their minds with superstition."

She clucked her tongue and shook her head in mock dismay. The magpie mimicked her.

"Such terrible things I do. When the pox strikes your small

nephew in three days' time, where will his anguished mother go? I should turn her away?"

A vein throbbed in his neck. He played to the crowd, gesturing to them. "You heard, she cursed him."

"No curse. It's in the cards." She shuffled her deck. When she stopped, she pulled a card from the middle without looking at it and placed it on the table. It showed a boy lying on a bed, pale as a ghost. A distraught woman looked on, wringing her hands.

The bailiff's great head swelled and crimsoned, like it would explode. "Enough," he thundered. He yanked the yellow cloth, spilling her wares into the dirt, and then over-turned her table. "I'll drag you to the stockade by your feet."

For a moment, a storm might have flashed in her eyes. She knelt and began gathering her cards, which seemed to fly into her hands.

"All I ask is to show my things in peace," she muttered. "Where would you have an old woman go?"

He began to turn away and cupped his hands to call for his sergeant.

She rose. Her bony finger shot out. "Stay."

He froze.

She began shuffling again. Her voice hardened. "Let's see what the cards hold for Bailiff Dunstable."

He faced her again, his eyes fixed on the cards with morbid curiosity.

She plucked a card randomly from the deck and held it up for him so he could see. "Ah, The Moon," she said.

He stared at the card. Painted in colored inks, a full moon shone in the night sky.

She tapped the card. "Tonight, you will have a visitor, the three-headed one. Do you know him?"

Pale, he shook his head like a man in a trance.

"He guards the gates to the underworld," she continued. "Mend your ways, Bailiff, or he'll drag you there."

He tried to speak but only croaking escaped his lips. The lines on the picture began to shift, curling and twisting as if an artist were applying inks on the spot. A cave formed at the base of a mountain, then a three-headed dog appeared before the opening. Little by little, it reared from the surface of the card and began walking round and round. Its tail swished and it lifted its three heads and six eyes fixed on him. A moment later it melted back into the card until it looked as it first appeared.

The bailiff staggered back. "Witch, you'll burn if you return."

He lurched off, thrusting people aside in his haste to flee the market.

The show over, the crowd moved on. A single boy remained, staring at her with eyes wide with astonishment.

Charna Diyna waved him over. "Come, little man."

He stepped forward bravely and stood before her.

"What did you see on the card?" she asked.

"A great bird over a house. It spread its wings like this." He held his arms straight from his sides and flapped them slowly.

"That was an angel, sweet one. It's going to protect you."

"It will?" His eyes grew as round as coins.

"You're Bailiff Dunstable's nephew?"

He nodded. "You know me?"

"How could I not know a beautiful face like that? But listen, in three days you will grow hot. Odd red marks will erupt on your skin. You'll have strange dreams. But don't be frightened. Soon you'll be chasing girls and pulling their braids again. All right?"

"All right."

"Give your mother this. When the spots appear, tell her to brew a tea with it." She handed him a packet of folded paper.

She mussed his hair. "When you grow up, you'll become

bailiff. You'll be kind and loved by all." She looked him in the eye. "Especially old women who visit the village."

She sighed and waved him away. "Go, I'm tired now."

As he ran off, she called after him, "Don't forget that packet."

When he was out of sight, she knelt and picked up her potions, still lying in the dirt. She put them in a sack with her cloth.

Business was slow. No one would be sick until tomorrow. With her things safely stowed in a gunnysack, she left the village.

It was rumored she lived in a hut deep in the forest, or a cave, or the pickled carcass of an elephant. No one had seen where she laid her head. It was surely under a bridge when it rained and under the stars when the night was clear.

The bailiff walked quickly from the marketplace and entered a warren of narrow backstreets and narrower alleys. The image on the card clung to him like a spider web. What could it have been but sleight of hand or some vapor she'd gotten him to inhale? Substances from the East were rumored to conjure visions. More likely it was a bit of haze on his mind, indigestion from too rich a meal, or drinking too deep from his cup.

The cold finger at the back of his neck withdrew.

Stopping at a back alley where fire had left a ruin of charred and jagged walls and caved-in roofs, he judged the time by the length of the shadows and fingered his money pouch. The stench of refuse flung from windows farther up the lane made his stomach twist. He sighed, for he loved his stomach above all else and hated to see it suffer. No matter, this little errand would soon be over. He would indulge his appetite on an entire goose pie, topped off with cranberry compote. His mind roamed over the bottles in his cellar and selected just the one to chase the meal down.

A few minutes later, the skeletal form of the apothecary slid up beside him.

The bailiff pulled a silk handkerchief from a pocket and patted perspiration from his face. "You're late."

The apothecary wrung his hands. "We was listenin' to talk, we was. We didn't like what we heard."

"You'd do well to pay no attention to wagging tongues."

"Maybe they wags the truth. They say Diyna the Witch was in the market."

"I don't deny it." Dunstable fingered the money pouch on his belt. "If she shows up tomorrow, she'll find herself spitted over a fire."

The apothecary's lips pulled back, revealing broken and missing teeth. "So you said before, but here she is, and didn't we already pay you?"

"She's testing me. She'll learn who her master is."

"She must." The little man clasped and twisted his bony hands. "Or she'll ruin us."

The bailiff gave a dismissive wave. "You have nothing to fear."

"They say she made a card come alive."

"A trick." The bailiff scowled.

"You don't believe in witches and warlocks?"

"I believe in swords, whips, and gold. That's what runs the world. For the rest, if you look deep enough, you'll find a man, not spirits, behind it. If someone tries to hoist one over me, Lord help him, I'll latch my hands around his neck."

"Or hers," the apothecary said pointedly.

"Or hers." A vicious smile spread across the bailiff's face. "I kept my part of the bargain. She left for a year." Flames burned in the bailiff's black eyes. He pulled his purse from his belt and jingled it. "Time for another payment."

The apothecary withdrew three silver coins from his

pocket. Before dropping them in the purse, he fixed the large man with his eyes. "Make her disappear, Bailiff, or we may find a shortage of catswort—yes, we might."

When the apothecary left, the bailiff ground his teeth, thinking how unpleasant it would be to go without catswort. He relied on it to ease colic. But he hefted his purse and the ring of the coins soothed him.

He glanced around to make sure no one had lurked and watched his transaction. All seemed well, but a magpie alighted on the edge of what had been a wall and began to strut side to side, shrieking at him.

"It can't be the same one," he muttered. He picked up a chunk of wood from the ashes. Putting his weight behind the throw, he sent the bird flying.

As its squawks faded, a dog slid from the ruins and whimpered up at him. It was nothing but skin and bones.

"Scat!" the bailiff said.

Instead of leaving, it sat and regarded him with woebegone eyes.

"No room in Wyebury for strays." With a sharp kick, the bailiff sent the thing yelping and scampering away.

As he ambled home, his skirmish with Charna Diyna was fading like a bad dream, and visions of goose pie, small potatoes, and baby carrots rendered in pig fat played in his mind.

The day started poorly but now was ripe as rain. One look at the lord's castle confirmed this. It rose before the bailiff, unassailable in its stone battlements. His position was quite to his liking. The lord visited once or twice a year. He left the management of his estates to his steward, who came here about as often as the lord. For his part, the steward left the day-to-day management of the manor, its lands, and the peasants who toiled on it to the bailiff. Almost the year round, this left the castle, its hall, its stores, its servants, and most especially its fine cellar, for his personal use.

He went up the road with a lively step and was about to pass the outer gate when a boy on crutches hobbled from behind the trunk of an old yew tree and called to him.

"Well, what is it?" the bailiff grumbled.

"Far and wide," the child began, when he stood before the bailiff, "The lord of Wyebury Castle is known for generosity. I had to come." The boy's clothes were nothing more than rags, stitched together crudely. Big holes in the breeches revealed that one of his legs was shriveled.

The bailiff waved him away. "There's nothing for you here."

"I know I don't look like much, but I can do things—milk a cow, churn butter, knead your baker's bread." The boy looked up at him with the longest lashes, framing eyes wide with hope.

"Where are your parents? They should be flogged for letting you wander."

"I never knew them, sir. I've been a traveler on the roads and byways as far back as I can remember."

"You mean a beggar. Run along. All our positions are filled."

The boy hesitated, glancing at the great, empty sky.

"Well, what's keeping you?" the bailiff asked.

"It's the nights, sir. They get terrible cold." He held his arms out, balanced on his crutches. "Might you spare an old coat or blanket? This is all I own in all the wide world."

"I don't think so," the bailiff replied coldly. "If I give to you, I'll have to give to everyone. Move along, or you can shiver in the stockade."

The child sank to his knees. "Mercy, good lord. What will I eat? I've had nothing for days."

"Eat? Why, you should eat grass, like the slow-witted calf

you are." With the boy's sobs in his ears, he turned and continued on his way.

"Insufferable creature," he said to himself. "Worse than the dog." And he laughed heartily all the way into the castle.

Soon he was settled in the great hall, resuming pleasant thoughts. For in reality, he *was* as good as lord of the manor. The family pennants on the walls could be his pennants. The armor, the swords, the maces, could be his weapons. The rich tapestries, the massive log crackling on the hearth, the servants who did his bidding—all were as good as his.

He poured a bumper of ale and toasted the lord and steward. "May you stay healthy, wealthy, and away."

A manservant entered carrying a tray, his face as pale as chalk. After he set the goose pie and its accompaniments before the bailiff, his eyes darted anxiously about the hall and pried into all the shadows.

"What the devil's wrong with the fellow," the bailiff muttered when the man had left. "Perhaps I'm too lenient on these creatures. A taste of the stick is good for them now and then. Reminds them to be quick and mind their place." Come to think of it, he thought, he should take such an implement with him to the market tomorrow morning. A few blows across Charna Diyna's back would solve all his problems.

He laughed long and hard, and the thought added spice to his meal. As he finished one plate after another, he imagined all kinds of tortures he could put her through.

Done eating at last, he began daydreaming about dinner. It was a way he had of working up an appetite. The wine and heavy meal soon had him snoring.

When he wakened, the fire had burned low. With a yawn and a stretch, he extricated himself from the chair and walked to the window. The sun was low in the sky. This was his favorite time of day. All his lands from the vineyards to the waving grains of barley were bathed in gold.

Crack! Crack, crack!

Startled, he jumped, and then laughed at his folly. 'Twas only the last of the log breaking and sending sparks up the chimney.

As he looked out the window again, a motion below caught his eye. The comely chambermaid, Janet, and the groom, Foster, were exiting a side door. He might have thought they were out for a tryst, but they appeared to carry knapsacks, as if for a journey.

The rumblings of his stomach turned him away with a shrug. What they did on their own time mattered not to him. He returned to the table and rang for dinner.

Seated with fork in one hand and knife in the other, he was surprised to see the head housekeeper approach with his meal, not the manservant.

"Where's that skulker?" the bailiff growled.

"Gone, sir," the housekeeper replied, arranging the steaming plates before him.

"Gone? Where to?"

"I don't know."

The bailiff threw down his napkin. "Turn him out. Leave his family, though. Let them meditate on their lazy relation."

"I expect he's long gone, sir. The other servants have left, too."

He almost shot from his chair, no mean trick for a man of his girth. "Left! What do you mean, left!"

"Run off, sir."

He sank back to the cushioned seat and rubbed his beetle-black brows. "Whatever for? They're fed and kept warm, aren't they?"

"They are, sir." She regarded him with an honest, forth-right gaze. "They heard, sir."

"Heard? Heard what?"

"The story ... What Charna Diyna showed you."

"Oh, that," he grumbled. "Bunch of superstitious fools, the lot of you."

"All the same, sir, I couldn't hold them if I threatened them with the pillory."

"What of you, Mistress Copeland?" He sneered. "Are you preparing your exit?"

She began to back away. "Will there be anything else, sir? A spot of tea? I've left the warmer on your bed."

He sank his great head into his hands. "No, this will do for now."

She was almost out of the hall when her words floated back to him, "Very good."

This strange turn of events almost spoiled his meal, but he soon lost himself in the glories of lamb chops, mint jelly, buttered peas, candied yams, and a decanter of fine claret.

Two sharp cracks from the hearth startled him from his revelry. A red glow was all that remained. A chill had settled on the large and drafty hall. No matter, it was time to light the candles and pour a glass of port. Mistress Copeland looked stout enough to throw a log on the fire. He rang the bell and waited. No sound of approaching footsteps echoed from the corridor beyond. He rang again, louder. The only answer was the house creaking as it cooled, for though it was faced with impregnable stone outside, its inner walls and rafters were made of wood.

Grumbling, he lit a candle and went off to investigate. A tour of the kitchen and servants' quarters convinced him he was quite alone. For a moment, a cold finger slid down the back of his neck. He shook it off, scolding himself for being a child.

He swore an oath and set off to get the port himself. In the candlelight, the corridors were dim and ghostly. Rustling came from behind. He glanced back, the candle throwing his long, deformed shadow on the wall and making it waver from a breath of cool air. He cupped his hand over the flame, lest the draft blow it out.

He reached the steps to the cellar and peered down. His

candle only penetrated a few feet—beyond was blacker than night. But a man must have port and port he would have. At the bottom of the stairs, the air was cold and heavy with must.

Click, click, click …

The sound was soft, faraway. It might have come from the floor above. Perhaps the wind was stirring metal curtain rings at an open window. After getting that log on the fire, he would have to go through the whole castle and shut all the windows.

Mistress Copeland and the others better have left for parts unknown. They would starve if they stayed in Wyebury.

The cellar was a long, stone tunnel beneath the castle. Rows of bottles ran from floor to ceiling on both sides, broken only by occasional kegs of beer, ale, and mead. He had no idea how deep the tunnel ran or what lay at the end, whether it was walled off, or simply narrowed into an apex of dirt. He set the candle down and began searching for the port, brushing away layers of dust and cobwebs that hung from the bottles like funeral drapes. Finding what he sought, he held up the bottle admiringly, and was just taking the candle up again when a tremor made tambourines of the bottles and sent a fine rain of dirt from the ceiling.

The bailiff wrapped a protective arm around the port. When the quake passed, he dusted himself and the bottle. As he turned to the stairs, a scratching sound came from deep within the cellar, as though someone were digging with a trowel. Unbidden, the image of a black pit at the back of the cellar formed in his mind. The hole grew wider, earth spraying into the cellar as if something were trying to break through the floor from below. A cold hand clenched his heart.

"Who goes there?" he called.

The scrabbling stopped. He held the candle up and ventured farther into the tunnel, peering into the shadows. He had no wish to go to the end. If one of the servants had come to drink in secret, he could spend a cold night here. So he convinced himself as he retraced his steps and passed up the stairs. But the image of the pit followed, and he could not shake it off until he'd slammed the door and locked it.

"They can rot there till morning." He laughed, but it sounded hollow in his ears.

In the great hall, he threw another log on the fire and then made a tour of the castle, closing and locking all the open windows. It seemed uncommonly dark outside, as though a black shroud had been stretched across the heavens, leaving cold and faint pinpoints of the stars. The wind whistled and rattled the shutters.

The library seemed just the place to enjoy the port. He settled into his chair before a warm fire, and was just about to take a sip, when he heard *click, click, click, click!*

He put the glass down, his face growing hot, and not from the fire. What had he said earlier? *If you look deep enough, you'll find a man, not spirits.* It was the servants trying to frighten him, or his sergeant trying to scare him off his job.

He bared his teeth. "Or Charna Diyna. Let her try. Let any of them try."

He rose, took up the fire poker, and stood in the doorway. A long hallway stretched to his left and right. The sound came from the left, like the nails of a dog striking the stone tiles, pacing toward him. Holding the iron before him, he trod down the length of the darkened hall until it intersected another. Finding this one empty, hearing no more tapping nails, he returned to the library, got his candle, and lit the wall candles along both sides of the hall.

Back in his chair, he sat several minutes, glowering. One hand rested on the poker. "When I catch them ..."

He took up his glass at last and swirled the ruby liquid. He was about to take a sip when, from the corner of his eye, something seemed to move. He glanced around the room and at the empty doorway. Light and shadows from the fire danced on the walls, nothing more. Still, there had been enough strangeness for one day to warrant investigation. A quick glance down both ends of the hall assured him he was quite alone.

With a sigh, he sank back in his chair. No sooner was he seated than a new sound echoed through the castle. Another round of tapping he could take. Buttons could be used to simulate animal nails. This new sound was different: a human might come close, but never quite capture it.

Panting, from three mouths.

The bailiff's eyes grew round. Sweat, cold and clammy, soaked his shirt and trickled down his spine, and he could smell his fear.

Steeling his nerves, he investigated with the poker. The hall was clear, the house silent. He was about to return to the library, but small bright spots a few feet from the door caught his eye. He stepped over quickly to inspect them. A dozen raindrop-sized droplets lay on the surface of the floor. He glanced at the ceiling. It was dry. It wasn't raining, nor had there been a leak anywhere in the castle. But he knew as he stooped over the clear liquid that it was not water. The distinct odor of canine breath wafted up to him, as if just moments before a dog had stood there, panting, drool dripping from its moist, red tongue.

But if a dog had sat there, it was no ordinary dog. Vapor, thin and ghostly, wafted up from each droplet. Moments later, they evaporated, leaving small craters in the stone.

The bailiff staggered back. He gasped and coughed as doubt put a stranglehold on his neck. His mind raced. There must be an explanation. But reason fled for the first time in his life.

He ran back to the library like a beast was nipping his heels, and slammed the door. The lock had no key. He carried over a chair, leaned it against the doorknob, and backed away, watching the door.

His heart pounded like a drum. Sweat cascaded from his brow. He shook, as though from a terrible fever. He snatched the poker and held it before him, prepared to defend himself to the death.

Ten, fifteen minutes passed. All the air seemed to have left the room. The only sound was the rasp of his shallow breaths as he sucked the thin stuff into his throat.

Slowly, his heart calmed. He inhaled deeply. He reached for the port, and whatever it was he'd been prepared to dismiss as tricks of his mind started coming down the hall.

Click, click, click, click …

It stopped outside the door, sniffing, scrabbling, whining like a hound trying to reach its prey. The knob rattled as if something pawed it. The door unlatched and swung slowly inward, pushing the chair with it. The back legs scraped the floor and then stopped. Through an eighteen-inch gap in the doorway, a shadow slid across the floor, a thick neck supporting three enormous heads. The jaws opened. Three tongues lolled out. Three mouths slavered with three sets of fangs, and low growling came from just behind the door.

The bailiff's ears roared. The veins in his neck throbbed. His lunch and dinner rose in a horrible bubble and seared the back of his throat. He scanned the room, hoping beyond hope he'd find a secret passage previously unknown to him. But the bookcase didn't roll aside, and the one window in the library overlooked a three-story drop.

The growling ceased. The shadow withdrew. The clicking nails faded down the hall.

Stumbling to the wine on rubbery legs, he downed two quick glasses. He kept a vigilant eye on the door, but as nothing happened, the threads of reason began to pull together.

Had the encounter with Charna Diyna been a dream? Was he now trapped inside a terrible nightmare from which he would awaken?

Doubtful, he thought, as he paced to and fro before the fire. They're using props, life-sized dog puppets. Drops of acid. It must be. There's no other explanation. Monsters don't suddenly appear. Witches can't summon them. There is no underworld, no place guarded by a three-headed beast. There are no fiends except the ones told to children to frighten them into being good. That didn't work when he was a child. It wouldn't work now.

The fear that had strangled him with icy hands withdrew. There had to be an explanation. He would figure it out, and when he did, he would skewer the culprit.

Fortified by this thought and the wine, he strode resolutely from the room, the poker gripped in his hand, not for defense but for punishment. Terrible laughter burst from his lips.

"I'm coming for you," he bellowed. "Now it's *my* turn!"

In his other hand he carried a lighted candelabra, the better to find the miscreants—for he was certain now there must be more than one. How else could the sound of panting and growling be tripled?

Just outside the door, where they must have crouched to make the shadow, he found more droplets dissolving. He bent close and sniffed. Besides the foul, evil-smelling stink of it, chemical fumes assaulted his nose.

He smiled and nodded. "Acid."

He had to admit they'd planned it well, using Charna Diyna for the first act, then props and sounds for what followed. No matter, they would pay dearly. For all he knew, the apothecary was in on it: he might be tired of dropping coins in the bailiff's purse and figured there was enough business to go around.

Fine. If the apothecary survived *him,* he would put up triple in silver. The thought cheered the bailiff like bright sunshine, more than he'd felt all day. It inspired celebration. What better way than a few slices of that joint of beef he saw in the pantry, and something delightful to wash it down.

A tour of the castle to find the villains, an expedition to the cellar, a trip to the pantry, and he would make merry in the great hall. Why, he could even sit on one of them.

His investigation of the lord's and lady's chambers, the towers, walkways, and battlements proved long and arduous. Nothing turned up. They'd left. That was the only explanation. There was nothing more to do but find a good merlot in the cellar, slice that slow-roasted beef, and head to the hall.

He froze at the cellar door. His head spun. The candelabra almost slipped from his fingers. Swallowing, he stepped forward to inspect. The door lay in pieces, shattered as though something powerful had forced past it. For a full minute he stared, trying to comprehend what he was seeing. It made no sense. He would have heard an explosion, or ax blows. Try as he might, no logical explanation came.

That left the unthinkable. He would not accept it. He would not.

Charna Diyna could do it. She'd tricked his eyes this morning. Perhaps one of her powders could silently rip a door to shivers.

Satisfied with this explanation, he nonetheless backed away, feeling a little more sober and a little less adventuresome. He would find something to quench his thirst in the servants' quarters or some corner of the kitchen.

He never made it that far. The passage outside the pantry was littered with food as though a raiding party had descended on it. A sack of flour was torn open. An enormous round of cheese was smashed like it had been hurled against the wall. Loaves of bread were gnawed apart. Baskets of beans, fruit, and eggs were overturned. Butter from the butter vat was smeared on the floor. Salted salmon had been dragged toward the great hall, from which a strange din arose: snuffling, scrabbling, chewing, a chair overturned, goblets rolling and dropping on the flagged floor.

Has the whole village gone mad? Have they stormed the place? The words were hollow. Doubt blossomed in the pit of his stomach and flowed into his veins, a dark and terrible tincture, freezing as it spread. He gripped the candelabra as if feeling something real would keep him from becoming unhinged. But his heart seemed to have grown and grown, pushing all aside until it filled every corner of his chest and pounded like a kettledrum.

"It can't be, it can't be—they're playing with me, playing with me." He repeated it over and over like a chant. It bolstered him enough to cautiously follow the trail of food, the raucous sound ahead becoming louder. Beside a standing suit of armor, he put down the candelabra and took the battle-ax from the gauntlet. The keen-edged weapon encouraged him to creep forward.

He began a new chant under his breath. "There are no witches, there is no magic, there are no witches, there is no magic."

Nearing the entrance to the great hall, he raised the ax. He had only to peek past a column, to which a patch of coarse white hair stuck, inches from his nose.

"There are no monsters."

Bit by bit, he leaned, until the entire room came into view. Curtains had been torn from the windows, tapestries from the walls. The bailiff's own chair was tipped over, one leg broken. The tablecloth was half pulled from the table, which was heaped with roast boar, a haunch of venison, herring, coneys, and pigeon, enough to feed the king for a week. A bottle spilled ruby wine on the floor. A giant hound sat amidst the food, six feet from paw to withers. From a tree trunk of a neck, three heads sprouted. One was buried in mince pie. A second gnawed a leg of mutton. The muzzle of the third was smeared with mint jelly. Saliva dripped from its dangling tongue and sent up fumes as it burned the table and floor. Its lips pulled back in a terrible grin, exposing six-inch fangs.

One head lifted from the pie. The second dropped the mutton. With a single bound, the creature was before the bailiff and grew until its ears brushed the rafters. The battle-ax slipped from the bailiff's fingers and banged on the floor.

He fell to his knees. "Mercy! Mercy!"

The six eyes staring at him were cold pools. Mirrored in them he saw the bony stray he'd kicked, which asked for nothing but a kind pat and a place by the fire; and the boy on crutches with the sweet, pleading eyes, who asked for nothing but work and a coat against the night's chill.

The bailiff shot up, whirled, and dashed for the front door, the hot breath of the beast on his neck.

Next morning, the first cases of pox appeared. When Charna Diyna arrived at her table, a queue had already formed to purchase her remedy. It wasn't a long line, but in three days, as fevers mounted and those who patronized the apothecary didn't get better, the number of people who sought her help grew. Because her cure worked, it wasn't long before the apothecary packed his bags and moved on to the next village.

The little boy the witch had given the packet to was the first to recover. Soon he was chasing girls around the market-place. More than one taunted him to pull her braids, for he was a comely lad. At eighteen, he became bailiff, and ruled with a fair hand. Whenever Charna Diyna arrived with her potions and powders, he set her up under an awning he reserved for her; she had shade in the summer and shelter from the rain in the winter. No one was surprised. He treated everyone with kindness.

The skin-and-bones dog found a friend in the boy on crutches, who was given a position in the kitchen. He shared his meals with the dog, and before long they both filled out nicely.

As for Bailiff Dunstable, he was never seen in the village again. Some claimed he became a brigand on the highways, which made sense since he'd been robbing for years. Others said a beggar roamed the countryside, raving that a great hound would drag them all to the underworld.

What is known is that soon after the bailiff disappeared, Charna Diyna set up her table in the marketplace of a nearby village. A crowd looked on as the local bailiff, a man with the look of a wasp, sent her potions flying into the dirt.

"Let see what the cards hold for Bailiff Stockman," she said in reply. She pulled out The Moon card and held it for all to see. The ink on the picture ran like tears. Curling, twisting, the colors formed a cave at the base of a mountain, then a three-headed dog, then a man, broad in the middle, with beetle-black brows. Little by little, these figures reared from the surface of the card. Round and round the card they went, the man running, the dog chasing. Owing to the man's girth, he was easy prey. One of the dog heads latched on to the back of his neck and dragged him to the cave.

Before disappearing inside, he looked out at the world, screaming, though no sound came.

THE WILLOW PRINCESS

*O*nce there was a queen, wise, beautiful, and beloved by her people. In the prime of life she married a soldier who coveted the power and riches of her kingdom. He was handsome and charming, and at first she was happy. But soon he dropped the pretense of civility and his selfish and greedy nature became evident. He left her alone and spent the day hunting or drinking in taverns. He told her she was someone no one could love. He spoke to her little. When he did, he belittled her edicts, told her what laws needed to be enacted, and demanded she raise taxes on the poor. As the months passed, she grew unhappy and weak. When at last she went into labor, she gave birth to twins and then promptly expired without ever seeing their faces. Had she lived a little longer, she would have been told that they were born holding hands, and bore identical crescent-moon birthmarks where those two palms met.

Since there were no other heirs but these two baby girls, the soldier proclaimed himself king. As he cared little for children, he ignored them utterly, and ordered their nursemaids to keep the two bawlers from his sight. The one time he saw them he flew into a rage, for one infant's hair was composed of long leafy vines, while the other, sure to equal her mother in radiance, reminded him too much of the wasted creature who had been his wife. Despite his neglect, they grew into sweet and kind children, and wherever they went, they were seen holding hands.

One day, the king came upon a crone who told him his fortune. "Your daughters will overthrow and banish you from the kingdom," she warned. He was not one to believe in prophecy, but the woman's words nibbled and burrowed at his mind like hungry maggots. Tormented beyond bearing, he found the crone and asked what he should do.

"Take them to the enchanted wood," she said, telling him where to find it. "The trees will do the rest."

Trusting no one else to do the job, he tore the leafy-haired daughter from the clasping hand of her sister. As he took her away, they both cried, "I'll find you, sister!" He bore her to the enchanted wood and left her at the knees of a stunted willow. Then he sat, and didn't have long to wait. The willow reached with branches like snakes, snatched up the sobbing child, and stuffed her into its trunk. The next instant, she was gone.

The remaining sister he thought he might sell to the highest bidder when she came of age, for who tosses away a jewel without getting a good price? With this in mind, he slapped chain-mail gloves on her hands and snapped a lock on each of them. Then he put her into the hands of an old, dull-witted miller on the edge of the kingdom, and paid him handsomely to keep the child there.

The girl grew into a beauty, and became a joy in the miller's life. She rose early and finished her chores early, despite the cumbersome gloves, which rattled and jingled everywhere she went. She helped him get the best prices for his flour at market, churned the butter, and kneaded dough with too big spoons, so the gloves wouldn't get gummy. When she wasn't occupied with work, she roamed the meadows and woods near her home, and soon birds, foxes, deer, and rabbits came running at the ringing music of her approach.

While her days were filled with wonder and delight, she could not say she was happy. An unaccountable emptiness and longing hung over her, for the moment the willow swallowed her sister she forgot she had one, and the hand with the crescent-moon birthmark withered. She asked the miller who her parents were and why she wore the gloves. If he knew, he wouldn't say, and only told her she must have committed a crime for which she was being punished. With a sigh, she scoured her memory for sign of what she might have done. All she found were large round eyes that seemed to implore her, and the hollow feeling that she had lost something important—and sometimes at night, she thought she heard a voice on the wind, calling her. Then she burrowed under piles of blankets and shivered, as if the ceiling of the house had been ripped away, and rain, snow, and the chill night air wrapped cold fingers around her.

Strange dreams troubled her. She wandered lost in a dark, forbidding wood. It seemed a rough, hard hand was pressed over her mouth, smothering her. She found a beautiful willow tree, with leaves that fell like the tresses of a princess, and she heard a child crying. Before she wakened, it seemed someone whispered in her ear, *Find me, sister,* and she reached out, as if to clasp something, someone.

As she neared her sixteenth birthday, the good miller fell ill and died. With no one to answer to, she ventured far from home, and the voice of her dreams began calling by day, soft, insistent. She followed its urging, which grew louder when she went one direction and softened when she turned another. Little by little, it drew her to a dark wood, where sticky spider webs snared her. But the birds came flying at the jingle of her gloves and chewed her free. The voice urged her on, and she plunged into quicksand. But the rabbits came and tunneled beneath the mire and drained it. Then the trees fanned up a gale against her. But the foxes came and draped themselves over her, and kept her warm until the storm passed. Then dense fog rose, and all around the trees bent and twisted, blocking her way. But she climbed on the back of a stag and rode it to safety.

On she ventured, and at last, in the darkest part of the wood she came upon the willow of her dreams. Tall and strong it stood, and now the voice called, *Free me, free me.* The voice was so plaintive, she thought her heart would break, but what she was to do and how she was to do it was as nebulous as fog.

Hold my hand, the voice urged.

She walked round and round the tree, looking for a hand. All she saw was the lustrous green hair of the willow.

Command the tree to give up its secret, the voice sang.

"Tree," she cried, "give up your secret." But look as she might, she saw no hand to hold.

Command the tree as its sovereign princess.

This confused her, but in a stout voice, she called, "As your princess, I command you to give up your secret." Still nothing happened.

Command the tree to give up your sister.

"Tree," she cried, in a good strong voice, "give up my sister!"

To her surprise, the long green tresses parted, revealing a withered branch with a curious crescent moon on it. She clasped the spot with her own withered hand. Warmth rushed up her arm. The locks snapped open. The gloves dropped away. The trunk burst asunder, and out stepped a radiant young woman. In a flash, she recognized the woman as her own dear sister, and all the memories of their childhood came flooding back. They clasped each other tight, and the instant their withered palms met, they were healed.

Hand in hand, they strode from the forest. They knew the magic was in them. Magic when they were together. Magic to face the future.

Magic enough to challenge the king.

THE DEMON MONKEYS

*S*camp's first sight of the wizard was in the village square, though at the time she only thought of him as the stranger. High up in the mountains, strangers were rare in Pin-Shoba, especially in the dead of winter when snowstorms blocked the roads and passes. But this man was different—he was making a large copper coin appear or vanish in his hand, behind a boy's ear, in a girl's pocket. A dozen children formed a ring around him. Every time Scamp tried to worm her way between them, they locked shoulders or shoved her back, sending her rolling into the snow. At last, she scooted between the legs of a tall boy, Mussen, and sat in the front where she could see everything that was happening.

The man wore a thick overcoat. Snowflakes caught and glistened like fireflies in his long white hair, and his beard floated lightly in the wind. His hands were delicate, the fingers long and nimble. Weary wrinkles troubled his face. When his sky-blue eyes fell on Scamp, they seemed to penetrate to the very bottom of her, and then probed at her tangled black mane, the rags on her back, her bare dirty knees, and the bare toes escaping scraps of cloth, her only footwear. She started to draw back in alarm, but merry laughter leaped into his eyes, and the next thing she knew, she was laughing and clapping as he found a sweetmeat behind her ear.

The crowd cheered for more. He obliged, drawing a rose from thin air—a rose in winter!—and then more astonishing: a small bird that hovered and beat a flutter-wind before winging away through the falling snow. The children pleaded for an encore, but he held up his hand and asked where he could buy rice, a few vegetables, and perhaps some beans. The village could spare little, but Scamp pointed out the hut of a farmer whose crops had fared a little better. He gathered up a shabby bag, hoisted it over his shoulder, and tramped in the direction she'd pointed. Something in her heart seemed to pull after him, but three of the taller boys hemmed her in.

"Give it over, Scamp," said Mussen, pimples swelling red and angry on his face.

She clutched the prize to her heart. "It's mine."

Scowling, Mussen bent low until they were almost nose to nose. "Was yours." Though she kicked at his shins, he pried open her fingers and dug the candy from her clasping palm, holding it out of reach. With his other hand, he shoved her into the snow.

Small, no older than six, there was little she could do but watch as they laughed and paraded from the square like the victorious soldiers of an invading army. The pangs in her belly proved more urgent than the sting to her pride. Having eaten little since last night, and less since the day before, she needed that sweetmeat. There was nothing to be done but go begging door to door. After dusting snow from her clothes, she made the rounds. Farmer Anskar had a healthy cow— perhaps he could spare a cup of milk or a bit of cheese. All she received was a scowl. His neighbor slammed the door in her face. And Tu-tu gathered up his few loaves and cakes and whisked them away. She met much the same through the circle of shacks, as she did most days. But old widow Kell gave her the kindness of advice. "Move on," she grumbled.

"We don't have enough for ourselves." And snapped shut her shutters.

The moving part of this counsel served well, for it kept her warm and occupied until the sun set. Under cover of absolute darkness that enveloped the village, she slipped past the houses like a wraith, longing to be inside one of them. Through the windows, she could see the happy faces of children, lit by a small candle or the warmth of firelight.

She left the homes behind and trundled up an icy path, passing fields promising a meager harvest, until she came to steps. She passed up them silently. At the top, she paused and peered intently into the shadows beyond the tremulous light of torches set around the perimeter of a clearing. No one lurked in the cedars shrouding the sides or stood at the altar nestled against the sheer side of a boulder. Satisfied the place was deserted, she crossed the clearing.

Carved in bas-relief in the stone behind the altar, howling monkeys leered with enormous round eyes that seemed to follow her. She half-expected them to spring to life and tear her to pieces. That they hadn't done so before did little to reassure her. Neither did the monkeys baying in the forest, their cries and wails raising cold hackles down her spine. Hunger urged her past her fear. In the great dish of the altar, the villagers had left offerings—little bowls with a spoonful of sticky rice, blackberries, a smallish dumpling, a finger of flatbread, and a few lentils.

After another scan of the trees satisfied her that she wasn't observed, she wolfed the meal down. The screech of the monkeys rose up as if in objection, spurring her from the clearing. The sound haunted her all the way back to the village. A short time later, she stole into farmer Naden's barn, relieved to be out of the biting wind. In one of the stalls, she huddled her frozen body against his sleeping goat, Dingle, drawing a complaining bleat. She told herself to awaken before dawn, or Naden would rouse her with a willow switch, and as Dingle warmed her, and a blanket of sleep began to slip over her, she thought of the stranger and imagined that he kissed the crown of her head.

A week passed before she saw him again, talking to widow Kell. The old woman clutched a straw broom as if she were ready to swing it as a weapon.

"No, I don't have peas or barley," she said. "No, I don't know who does."

He jingled a leather pouch and showed her the contents.

"It wouldn't matter if it was gold instead of copper," quoth she. "Let me offer a bit of advice—we have no use for conjurers here, unless you can conjure a full larder."

He did no better at the next house. The owner told him to try a neighbor or the next village. The eyes of a third narrowed with suspicion, while a knot of men watched the stranger from behind a corral and skulked away when he approached. Scamp followed him through the village, peeking from an alley or from behind a wagon. At last, giving up the entirety of his pouch, the stranger managed to get supplies from one of the farmers.

As he loaded rice, beans, and a few limp vegetables into his sack, he asked, "What can you tell me about the little girl with no shoes or coat, the one with the mop of tangled hair and dusty knees?"

Hearing him describe her, Scamp edged closer.

"Scamp?" the farmer replied.

"Has she no family, no one to take care of her?" asked the stranger.

"We help as we can." The farmer backed into his house and began closing the door, until it was open only a crack. "Stay clear of her. She's cursed."

The farmer's words passed by like clouds, for the stranger's questions bathed her in bright sunshine. He'd thought of her! Her, little Scamp! At that moment, he might have bent and planted that kiss on her crown. Her heart swelled. She floated, dizzy with pleasure.

He was stepping off, taking the lane out of the village. She couldn't let him out of her sight! Darting after him, she went from tree to tree so she wouldn't be seen. He strode quickly, leaning against the wind. They passed the fields, blanketed in white, and entered a tall stand of cedars. She looked apprehensively about her as howling rose in the distance. It began to snow, and he turned onto the path leading up the mountain.

No! she thought, and fear wrapped icy fingers around her throat, for she had never ventured this far from the village, and it was said these woods were home to the demon monkeys. But the stranger seemed to tug on her heart and she plodded on.

Snowflakes whirled, eddied, and billowed about him. At times, he seemed to fade behind a white veil, and she hurried her steps so she wouldn't lose him. Snow piled up on both sides of his tracks, but did not fill the deep impressions of his footprints. Once, the two of them followed nothing more than a thin trace on a sheer rock face that dropped into roiling clouds. At last, the path leveled off. They passed for a time through a stand of tall and silent trees and came out on a perch near the top of the mountain.

The flurries parted before him as he followed a path that led to a hut. The roof sagged. The walls were old and weathered. No smoke curled from the stone chimney, no light, warm and inviting, poured from the windows. He paused, perhaps to catch his breath from his journey, and then trod up a narrow track into the hut.

Scamp watched as a lantern flared within, then she crossed the open space, hopping like a rabbit from drift to drift so she remained unobserved. She stopped near a fallen fence and sucked in a breath in astonishment. Snow piled in small mountains around the hut, flurries swirled all around it, but none fell on the roof, windowsills, or doorstep. What's more, blue and yellow flowers pushed through the white blanketing the yard and nodded gently in window planter boxes.

She crept to one of the windows and peeped through the shutters. A ponderous book lay open on a wooden table. Arranged on a bench were objects she didn't know the use of —tubes and triangular bottles of clear crystal, filled with colorful liquids. A loom sat in one corner, a spinning wheel in the other. Two chairs, a tired rug, and a narrow bed covered with a thin blanket composed the rest of the furnishings. Strange, flowering plants hung from the ceiling. Logs waiting to be lit were stacked in the fireplace.

He rubbed his hands and flexed them to work out the cold and stiffness. Then he removed a small box from a shelf and opened it. Into his palm he shook out a small quantity of shimmering dust and blew it upon the cold hearth. The next instant, a cheerful fire sprang to life.

Turning his hands near the flames, he called out, "You've come this far, Sugarplum, you might as well step in where it's warm."

She looked about for Sugarplum, wondering who that might be. Then, with the thrill of a little bird, she realized he was talking to her. Still, after stepping shyly through the door, she stood shivering at the entrance until he waved her over to the fire.

She wondered how long she would be able to stay, for she had never felt this warm, not even when she slept with Dingle. "Why do you call me Sugarplum?" she asked.

He nodded in the direction of the village. "Better than what they call you."

She couldn't argue with that and decided she liked the name.

While she twirled her toes before the flames, he poured

water from a pitcher into an iron pot. With a knife, he began to cut carrots, leeks, and the meat of a bright red gourd.

"Where are your parents?" he asked.

She came over to help, scooping the diced vegetables into the pot. "They died."

"Why doesn't someone take you in?"

Her brow wrinkled as she puzzled it out. "They don't have enough food."

He stared at her. "Surely there's enough for one small girl."

"They can't keep it."

She would rather have left it at that, but he fixed his eyes on her and waited until she continued. For a moment, the blaze on the hearth seemed to waver and burn cold.

"It's the demon monkeys," she said, almost in a whisper. "They come on fire steeds and take everything."

He looked down at her sharply. "Have you seen them?"

"Their picture ... on the village altar." And she heard them in the woods. She told him they came when the snow began to melt, thundering down the mountain wrapped in flames. Then the villagers carried enormous baskets filled with grains, and took up armfuls of wool stuffs and boxes of porcelain with delicately fired glazes, for they were known for their intricate designs, and brought them to the demon monkeys.

"What if they refuse?" the stranger asked.

Scamp's eyes grew round with fright. "They'll burn the village."

The blood must have drained from her face, for the man began setting the table with wooden bowls and spoons and asked no more. Talk of the demon monkeys had brought snow into her bones, but the soup warmed her and her fear dissolved. Soon, she was prattling and laughing as if she'd never spoken about them.

After they ate, he sat before his book, studying the glyphs. From time to time, he traced an arc in the air with his finger and turned the pages without touching the paper. As astonishing as this was, it had been a long day and a long trek up the mountain, and presently, sleep tugged at Scamp's eyelids.

She rose. "I should go." Outside, the wind began to shake the windows and hiss about the cottage.

"Nonsense. It's almost dark and the storm is just getting its teeth." He stepped to the trunk at the foot of his bed and removed rolls of combed wool, ready for spinning. He unfolded yards of it near the hearth and stacked layers to make a bed. Over this, he threw his winter overcoat and tucked her in beneath it. The soughing wind seemed to fade. Just before the crackling flames lulled her to sleep, she saw him sit up from his book. His face glowed, his eyes almost burned as he murmured, "One more ingredient, then I can make it."

She came often to visit after that, for he was kind, and there was always a place to sleep by the fire and a hot meal to fill and warm her belly. She had a habit of asking questions, and once she got going, she had a hard time stopping. Old widow Kell scolded her often for it, saying her curiosity would kill a cat. The stranger—his name was Wyndano—made her more curious than anyone she'd ever met. He tapped a shell the size of a melon, and a soft, back-and-forth whooshing filled the cottage, and the air was permeated with an exotic aroma of plants and birds and fish, but not like those in the streams, and she was suffused with a sweet, exquisite longing for something she couldn't name. With a gesture from the wizard, his flute lifted into the air all on its own and began to bob and play a wistful tune. Wyndano was so strange and wonderful she had to know about him.

"Where do you come from," she asked, for he spoke with an accent.

He looked up from his book, which he had been engrossed in, and waved toward the west. "Far, far away."

Questions poured out, one after another.

"How long will you stay?"

"Why did you come?"

"What are you making?"

He frowned at the last one, and she worried that maybe she'd killed a cat. But he said, "All in good time, Sugarplum." He did tell her something of his travels, describing valleys painted with flowers, rivers that carved canyons, forests so dense you had to cut your path with a sword, and a place where land stopped and water as far as you could see crashed onto white sands.

He pointed to the shell that made the wonderful sound and scent. "That's where I got that."

She could hardly believe the world contained so much. As far as she knew, there was only the mountain. Hundreds of villages rested on its shoulders and ridges, but beyond that, the world plummeted into clouds. So said the elders. And most of the people in the village. But here was this stranger with strange ways and strange doings. Besides, she trusted him. If he said it was true, then it must be, and he knew so much more than any of the wise elders, who seemed like children compared to him.

But the question about what he was making, which had occupied her mind since that first night, he would not answer, nor would he say why he was there. But she worried about the cat and bit her tongue and tried to be as helpful as she could. Perhaps she'd get the answer by watching him, for he was almost always active. With a snap of his fingers, the candles below the crystal containers ignited. When the crimson, blue, and green liquids bubbled, he sprinkled them onto the rolls of wool.

"Do you know how to spin?" he asked.

No one had ever let her near a spinning wheel, but she had watched wool and flax get twisted into thread and thought she could do it. Seated at the great wheel, she held the fiber in her left hand and turned the wheel with her right. He adjusted the angle of fiber to spindle, and with a thrill, she saw she'd produced the necessary twist to make thread. After that, he left her to her work, though from time to time, he changed from wool to flax, from flax to silk, from silk to parts of trees, honeysuckle, and reeds, and sometimes, small portions of thin leather, animal tendons, and sinews found their way into the finished strands.

While she spun, she watched him work at the loom with her thread. He was slow and meticulous, sometimes pulling out a line and redoing it so that the weave was tight and the texture met his standards. Every so often, he sprinkled aromatic powders or colored liquid from one of his crystals onto the fabric, and he spoke strange words over it. She observed all this with rapt attention. What they were making, though, remained a mystery.

The path to getting this question and many others answered began at the village. One day, the wizard came in for supplies, and Scamp saw him talking to widow Kell. She wouldn't have spied on him, but she heard him pressing the old woman about what happened to Scamp's parents. She peeped from behind the trunk of a fir tree and heard all they said.

"Why is the village so cruel to the little girl?" the wizard asked.

"I can't see as it's any business of yours," Kell replied.

A sly smile came into his eyes. "Perhaps not, but I heard your best egg-layer ran off."

Kell folded her arms. "What of it?"

"Nothing really, just that she might come strutting and scratching back to you."

Kell glowered. "Fine." And Scamp heard the truth about her parents, how one year, the village almost starved because the harvest was given in tribute. How her parents imagined a better life, for they believed their lands could produce enough for everyone. How they tried to rally the village to fight the demons off. They refused. Everyone hid when the demons came, everyone except Scamp's parents, who faced them alone.

"They died like that," Kell said with a snap of her fingers. Their death confirmed the villagers' worst fears. The demons left them hanging on stakes for all to see and cursed the village, telling them that resistance would bring bloodshed. They pointed to the savaged bodies of her parents and said their offspring would be cursed, and whoever stood up to them again would be cursed, and their descendants cursed for ten generations—not to be touched, not to be cared for, lest ruin come to the village.

"Now, where's that chicken?" asked Kell.

Wyndano paled at this tale, but he twittered like a strange bird, and presently, a great leghorn sashayed around the corner, shaking its comb.

Wrapped in sadness at the fate of her parents, Scamp journeyed up the mountain. How foolish they'd been, and how courageous! It must have been a terrible winter, a meager harvest, for them to risk so much. And Scamp couldn't help but think about the murmurings and whispers of the villagers that this year was one of the worst they'd seen. Surely, they would starve. Fear and desperation filled their eyes and left them careworn.

But in the wizard's hut, Scamp's spirits always brightened. That night, she vowed it was time for answers.

"Wyndano," she ventured, "what are we making?"

He looked up from his loom, his shoulders suddenly tense. "Don't ask, Sugarplum."

"Why not?" she cried, tears springing to her eyes. "You asked widow Kell about me."

He gazed at her a long moment and sighed. "Very well. Perhaps it would be good to tell. I've spoken to no one of this and have carried it too long." He blew into his hands and rubbed them. "It grows cold. Come, sit by the hearth. We'll make tea and talk."

She brought over her chair while he stoked the fire and put a kettle over the flames.

"Like the people of your village," he began, "I was a farmer—like my father and his father before him, all the way back to dimmest memory. We were a carefree lot, working from sunup to sundown in the fields, and nothing gave us more pleasure than to see young shoots push from the black earth. The happiness of the day poured into the night, when we sang blessings to the gods, for our land was rich and the plants seemed to leap from the soil. I had much to be thankful for—a loving wife, whose raven hair flashed in the sun, and a daughter—" His voice broke. "—about your age. Tidings of war troubled us little—it was far away and not our affair. Little by little, though, a shadow reached toward us. Closer it came, bringing dark tales of a necromancer, whose army ravaged and destroyed all before it and enslaved the few who survived. Day by day, our terror grew, but we were a peaceful people, and what could we do with pitchforks and shovels?"

The water began to hiss and bubble. He brewed tea in a pot, and when they both were sipping from steaming cups, he continued. "For a time, it seemed they would skirt us. We had just begun to relax when they struck in the dead of night. The screams still echo in my ears. Our homes still burn red before my eyes. A falling beam must have knocked me senseless. I came to the next morning, buried beneath a fallen ceiling. I crawled from the rubble to find my village charred and tumbled to ruin. Frantic, I ran from blackened shell to black-ened shell of a house, searching the wreckage, calling my wife, calling my daughter. No one answered ... No one would ever answer."

He stared into the fire as if he saw blazing rooftops. It seemed to Scamp that he might float off. She held his big hand between her two tiny ones. At length, he gazed down at her and opened his arms, and she crawled into his lap, and he clasped and rocked her to his breast.

"I wandered, a dead man, caring little where I went," he continued at last. "When I wakened, I found the land unfamiliar. Still, I journeyed in a daze, with a vague idea I was traveling west. I crossed forests and vast sheets of frozen ice. I sat in tents with wise men, smoking pipes, sweating, chanting, breathing deeply of sage thrown on steaming rocks. A vision seized me—to seek teachers, sages, magi, anyone who could heal me. On I roamed, west, always west. I searched by rivers and deep in valleys. I found them in caves and on the highest mountains. Two or three were genuine and knew rare and beautiful enchantments. Years I apprenticed, absorbing, gleaning the best from each of them. They peered into my heart and told me the same thing—forgive, forget. I could do neither. They told me revenge would blacken my heart. That I heard, though at first there was nothing I could do about it. Gradually, gradually, though, a new idea formed, not for vengeance—for freedom. I would rise, more powerful than the necromancer, and overthrow him."

He sipped his tea and gazed at his weaving, still on the loom. It had grown long, but still he said it was incomplete.

"And here I am, Sugarplum, making what I need."

She gazed at the weaving in wonder. "What is it?"

His eyes were flames, though perhaps it was just a reflection from the fire. "A cloak, such as has never been seen in the world."

Here was a new puzzle. How would a cloak help him defeat the necromancer?

But all he would say was, "Soon, child, soon."

He made up her bed, for there was still plenty of unspun wool, and he tucked her in.

She looked up at his face, thinking for the first time that it was not only kind, but beautiful. "Wyndano, what do you need to finish the cloak?"

"Hair." He bent and kissed the crown of her head. "Of a hero."

His answer suddenly seemed unimportant. That evening, he'd held her in his arms. And now he'd kissed her. For as long as she could remember, no one had done either. Even as she fell asleep, the wonder of it filled her mind.

Winter began to wane, which was not reassuring on the mountain—the final storms were often the fiercest, and tribute day with the demon monkeys was drawing near. Wherever she went in the village, Scamp saw worry deepen on the faces of the villagers. As feared, much of the winter crop had failed. What would be given in tribute would be small and would anger the monkeys, who would punish them and take the little they'd kept. No one said it, no one had to, she could see it in their eyes—they would starve.

A series of storms kept Wyndano and Scamp bound to the cottage. Engrossed with his work, he gave it little thought. Instead, he worked feverishly on the cloak, dyeing it with liquids from his beakers, sprinkling it with powders, casting over it incantations and enchantments. But as his supply of food diminished, Scamp began to worry. She begged him to let her get a few things so he might finish the weaving. When the snow stopped and the sky cleared and the sun was unusually warm, he allowed her to return to the village for supplies. But he made her promise to not venture back if another storm came.

As she set out, she had no fear whether they would sell her what she needed. She'd been his proxy for some weeks, and as he'd proven to be helpful—the miraculous recovery of a sick cow, the return of a wandering donkey—even in these dire times, she always brought something back. So it came that Scamp was in the village shortly before tribute day. No one needed to tell her where they were in the phases of the moon and the tilt of the sun. She could see it in their drawn and anxious faces, and she heard it in their uneasy whispers.

She collected the few things she needed—a wedge of cheese, small sacks of flour, rice, beans, and a few condiments. She looked warily at dark clouds blotting the setting sun and decided to spend the night with Dingle. By the time she reached the barn, she sensed a change in the wind, which brought the scent of something cold and dark. Soon, gusts rattled the walls, and Dingle stirred and bleated apprehensively, and she wrapped her arms around him, trying to reassure him.

She was up with the sun and cast a worried eye toward the horizon. Clouds loomed. Like ominous towers they rose. A low rumble came, and the morning sounds of scratching chickens and pigs at the trough seemed to pause and then tremble. She hurriedly threw her knapsack over her shoulders and tramped through the village. Windows were shuttered— goats, cows, and horses were scurried into barns—babies were snatched up and rushed indoors. Farmers hastened in from the fields. Birds raced east.

Scamp gauged the distance to the clouds. There was time —she could reach Wyndano before the storm struck.

Just before slamming and bolting her door, old widow Kell called to her. "Hide, Scamp, hide while you can. They know! It's the demon monkeys, punishing us for a short tribute."

Scamp pressed on. The village fell behind her, the fields too, the fences blown down. A low drum roll rumbled down the mountain. Wind moaned in the cedars. The great trees swayed and whimpered. The leaves trembled. The branches rattled and shook. Icy gusts snatched at her knapsack, as if to tear it from her back.

Clouds tore across the sky. The sun seemed to shrink and then disappeared behind a black pall. Howling wind drove the first stinging flakes. Swirling, diving, spiraling, it blinded and taunted her, and she could swear the monkeys were in the midst of it, laughing at her. She came to a tree, toppled and half-buried like a giant in the drifts. Its enormous roots reared up like a hand, urging her to stop, urging her to return the way she came. Violent blasts sent snow streaming in curtains, and sky and tree and trail faded to white. On she forged, fingers numb, the constant whistling and shrieking in her ears, and she came again to the fallen tree, its roots twisted up in warning. But she leaned against the gale and at last found the track up the mountain.

Here, new perils waited. The trail narrowed to a thread clinging to near-vertical heights. Clouds billowed and boiled below, as if a chained monster thrashed inside to free itself. Her feet slid in the drifts. The wind threatened to lift her like a kite. The storm drew a shroud across her eyes, and instinct alone kept her from plunging off the mountain. The sky ripped. In one ruddy flash, she saw the mountain huddled like a child and black clouds stampeding down on it like wild horses. The next instant, an unearthly bellow struck the cliffs and crashed and echoed on the bluffs and crags. Again it came, low deep knelling, as if the whole mountain was a bell, and then a series of claps so terrible she wondered if the mountain was erupting and every boulder and stone above would come crashing down on her.

Less than a speck, less than one of the tiny flakes whirling in the wind, she staggered on, until at last she came to trees, a path, a garden with blue and yellow flowers poking up from a blanket of white, a door. It opened. Light streamed out. A man stood framed in the entrance. He was running now, sweeping her in his arms, carrying her inside, and the white withdrew, and she was wrapped in warm blackness.

She wakened beside a blazing fire, wrapped in his overcoat. A kettle of water was bubbling over the flames, sending up delicious steam.

He handed her a cup of tea. "This will take the sting from your fingers and toes."

It tasted bitter, but the redness and pain quickly faded, as did the worry in his eyes.

She tried to tell him she was sorry for disobeying him, but he hushed her. "The storm tricked us both," he said. "Had I known you were out there, I would have come for you. I thought you would wait it out in the village. How do you feel?"

She flexed her fingers and curled her toes. "Better."

His eyes sparkled. "Guess what I found behind the hut?"

She looked about the room with excitement and saw something big hidden beneath his blanket. He whisked away the blanket and revealed a five-foot-long tub made of hardened pottery. "I bet you've never had a hot bath."

She watched in amazement as he moved the tub beside the fire. He poured in boiling water from the kettle and then cooled it a little with snow. Then he hung the blanket as a curtain. Soon, she was immersed, and the most delightful heat soaked into her bones.

"Be sure to wash your hair," he called. "The storm made a rat's nest of it."

Too soon, she was out and dried and wrapped in his blanket. He handed her his brush. While she ran it through her hair, she told him about the village.

"Wyndano, I'm scared." She told him about the failed crops, how everyone looked apprehensively toward the altar circle, how widow Kell said the demon monkeys would punish the whole village for being short. "They're coming. Tomorrow night," Scamp said.

He pondered her a long time. Then he rose and took a large sheet of paper from his trunk and laid it out on his table with a brush and a few pigment inks.

"Show me what they look like," he said.

She painted as best she could, showing their icy eyes,

terrible grinning mouth, and yellow flames shooting from their heads. When she was done and the ink was dry, he showed her how to fashion it into a lantern and then hung it from the ceiling on a length of twine.

"No," she cried. "It'll bring them."

He handed her the big spoon he used to stir soup. "Break it."

She hesitated. Even her own crudely drawn image of them filled her with fright.

"Go ahead," he urged. "Right through the other side."

She swung, ripping through the monkey's nose. The bottom of the lantern tore and fell to her feet.

He picked up the fallen piece and threw it into the fire. "That's all they are, Sugarplum. Little more than paper."

She shook her head vehemently. "But I saw them. In the storm. Oh, if only the cloak was done, *you* could stop them."

He gazed at his loom—his eyes bright as flames. "We will. Together." He turned to her. "I found my hero."

Another surprise! she thought. *Like the tub. He's here!* Rippling with excitement, she scanned the room, prying into shadows near the trunk, the loom, the great spinning wheel, and beneath the bed. Where? Where was he?

Meanwhile, Wyndano took up the hairbrush she'd been using. He removed white tangles of hair lodged in the bristles and then carefully drew out two lustrous black strands.

"Spin them, Sugarplum, with wool and honeysuckle fiber."

Confusion must have played across her face. He laid a hand on her shoulder. "Many a man would have quailed before that storm. Fearing I would be trapped without supplies, you forged through it with the heart of a lion."

She barely felt them, barely comprehended their meaning, as he dropped the strands into her outstretched palm, though it dawned on her slowly as she began to spin. He meant her!

When she'd twirled it into yarn, he wove it into the cloak

and then removed it from the loom. He laid it out on the table and took up one of his sparkling powders, which he blew onto the material. She wasn't sure what was supposed to happen, but he held it up in the firelight, and she drew in a breath. Across the surface, mighty bears lumbered, cranes soared in misty valleys, great horned sheep roamed rocky crags, snow leopards prowled ravines, and iridescent fish swam silvery waters. Then yaks and horses, rabbits and mice, goats and antelopes, eagles and hawks came leaping, racing, darting, winging across the surface of the fabric.

"What does it do?" she asked in wonder. Now, creatures of myth and folktale shimmered on the weaving, fierce-eyed, streaming fire and smoke.

He gazed at his work, eyes alight. "Whatever you imagine. Do you trust me, Sugarplum?"

She smiled up at him, nodding.

"And do everything I say?"

She nodded again.

"Good. Tomorrow, we take care of your monkeys."

Midafternoon next day, Scamp and Wyndano strode into the village. Tense quiet replaced the usual hustle and bustle. No one gossiped by the fences and corrals. No children jumped rope, romped with a dog, or played catch with a gourd. No chickens pecked and scurried through the snow, and the paths between the houses were empty. Scamp wasn't surprised. On tribute day, people left the fields early. Last-minute preparations were made to fill baskets. And in some homes, small sacks of rice and barley were stealthily hidden under floorboards.

Even the air was still. But as Wyndano went from house to house, the new cloak hanging from his shoulders rustled as if a breeze stirred and lifted it softly. Birds, insects, reptiles, and animals no longer coursed across the fabric, yet Scamp knew they were there—waiting. At first, people would only listen to him from behind doors or shutters. But when he demonstrated the cloak, they stepped from their homes, astonishment on their faces. Soon, a crowd followed him.

Full darkness shrouded the edges of the clearing. This night, the moon would not rise. Light snow sprinkled down. It seemed to appear and disappear, blurring the clearing and dressing the trees in cold clothing. Half of the villagers lay hidden, spread out on both sides of the steps just below the top of the hillside. Standing beside Wyndano a few feet forward of them, Scamp sensed rather than heard the edgy whisper of them stirring. She guessed they were relieved Wyndano wanted them out of sight. She wondered if they would come out when they were needed. Everyone else was hidden in the village—in case the plan went bad.

A cold breath stirred the cedars. Wyndano leaned forward, listening, and the cloak billowed like the wings of an immense bird. A low rumble sounded in the distance. Far away, as if in answer, monkeys began to howl. Little by little, rather than fading, the thunder deepened, drumming, drumming, like an oncoming storm. And the din of baying and barking grew.

"Are you ready, Sugarplum?" Wyndano asked.

A lump rose into Scamp's throat, but she nodded.

"Good. Remember, do what I told you."

He dropped a white pebble then seemed to vanish. Scamp knew he was there, four feet to her right, and anyone looking might have seen a small black beetle crawling over the snow and then onto the pebble. She clutched a leather pouch in one hand. It felt uncommonly light.

The beating and pounding drew near, a terrible chorus

coming with it. Through the branches and leaves, something bright and ruddy flared, as if the trees had ignited.

Then they were there—a dozen of them, thundering into the clearing. Flames licked from the manes and tails of their steeds. Fire rippled along the arms, legs, and torsos of the riders, and a blaze, cold and blindingly bright, shot from their heads. One of them was head and shoulders above the others. His horse reared, pawing the air, and then its hooves crashed down into the snow. With pent-up energy, it stamped from side to side and then stepped a pace forward. The demon's hands were like huge stones. His broad shoulders and tree trunk of a neck supported a large, misshapen head. A wrinkled, bloated snout protruded from his face. His eyes flared with menace.

"So, the cowards send little girls now." He spat into the snow. "Where's the tribute?"

She swallowed against the lump in her throat. "It's not yours." Her voice seemed small and weak compared to the rough and booming sound of his.

"Not mine?" He laughed, and the riders behind roared with dark mirth. "Run along. Tell your parents to bring that tribute, or the village burns."

"No more tributes. Ever." She took a step forward, hoping they couldn't see her trembling, and pointed back the way they'd come. "Leave while you can or face your doom." Pride surged through her—she'd gotten Wyndano's words right.

"You little wretch, I'll roast you over flames and suck out your marrow."

He spurred his steed. When he was almost upon her, she reached into the pouch and pulled out a handful of winking dust, hurling it at him. Some of it landed on his legs and the horse's chest. In a blink, it spread over horse and rider and then over his followers, extinguishing the flames, sending up a sulfurous vapor, and revealing men wearing masks.

The leader bellowed and lunged for her. At that

moment, a new demon monkey appeared beside her astride a giant of a horse. He towered over the man. Unlike the fire of the men—which was cold—hot flames burst from his head and ran down his shoulders, arms, and legs, his long, white hair flying with fire. His face was crimson, his features outlined in black and gold, and his eyes glowed icy blue.

The leader's horse reared. Pale, eyes bulging, the man yanked the reins, urging his steed back. The next instant, the villagers leaped from hiding, brandishing shovels, pitchforks, axes, clubs, and hastily made spears. They spread out into a ready and determined line.

The demon raised his hand. A sword materialized in it and burst into flames. He whirled it, sending a hot gale before him. "Brigand, your days of stealing are over," he thundered. "A new god protects these people. Set one foot on this mountain and I'll ride you down." He pointed to Scamp and then several of the farmers. "Harm one such as this, or him, or her, and I'll find you where you hide and scatter your ashes to the winds. Go!"

That's all the urging they needed. Lashing their steeds, the brigands fled from the clearing. Head tilted, the demon gazed in the direction they'd gone. The beat of their horses faded. Still and silent he stood, and then in a wink, where the flaming horse and demon had been, there was Wyndano, his cloak rippling lightly in the breeze.

He nodded in the direction of the departing brigands. "If you follow them, you'll find a trail of bones," he said to the villagers. "They used them to draw snow monkeys from the forest. That's how the howling grew as the riders came."

"But the flames," one of them exclaimed. "It shot from their faces and horses."

Wyndano snapped his fingers. Fire leaped from his palm. "Mix certain chemicals and you get harmless flames. Magicians use it, though how those ruffians came by it, I don't know." He held it out to Scamp, who doused it with powder from her pouch.

"Go," he said. "Throw your doors and windows wide, and till your fields in peace."

Snow, which had danced and darted about him like fireflies, stopped falling.

~

Streams wakened. Rivers yawned and murmured. Shepherds led their sheep from snowy highlands into the valleys. Emerald and jade slopes swept down from snow-capped peaks. Honeybees gathered nectar from wild mustard painting the hillsides, and rhododendrons burst with blossoms. If her mountain contained all this, Scamp thought, what treasures might the rest of the world hold?

She turned back from the vistas and heights to gaze into the faces of the villagers, assembled on the main road leading down the mountain. They formed a ring around Wyndano, who tied his rucksack to the saddle of a horse they'd given him in gratitude. Scamp's heart was in a tangle.

He adjusted the bridle and then laid his hand on her shoulder. "What will you do for this girl?" he asked, addressing the crowd.

Anskar stepped forward with his wife and daughter. "We'll take you in. You'll have plenty of cheese and hot milk if you stay with me."

Tu-tu put an arm around his wife. "We've got bread and cakes, right out of the oven."

Naden wasn't married, but he said, "I'll give you Dingle. He follows you around anyway. You might as well have him."

Wyndano gazed down at Scamp, his eyes misty. "You could have a place, Sugarplum. Would you like that?"

"Where will you go?" she asked.

"You know where. Someone has an account to pay."

"I was thinking about the rivers and valleys," Scamp replied, "the deserts and the place where you found that shell. It would be something to see. And ... and ... You might need me, so you don't fight him alone." She bit back tears.

Widow Kell folded her arms. "Let me give you some advice, Scamp. Best to not get mixed up with conjurers."

Wyndano stepped into the stirrup and swung onto the horse. "What do you imagine, Sugarplum, what do you want to be?"

She looked up at him hopefully. "Your daughter."

He laughed. "You're that already." He reached down and drew her up in front of him. Together, they rode down the road, the world open and calling. As they receded, anyone watching might have seen them stop, as if to take in the view. Anyone looking might have seen the horse leap from the precipice, the cloak drifting upward, and where horse and riders had been, a giant bird soared and then vanished west in the twinkling of an eye.

TANGLES

*N*o one knows I have the book. They'll be mad when they find out. I don't know why. You told me you only did good things with it.

I came here by myself. No one notices as I walk through the big double doors with tall columns on both sides. The nurses don't look up. They're too busy behind their counter.

No one will miss me at home, not today, not any day. They're like the nurses, too busy to pay attention.

I walk past lots of old people. They're in wheelchairs, all pulled in with their chins glued to their chests. It scares me. You told me that your head would hang too, maybe by next Christmas. One of them looks at me and tells me she needs the bathroom. The hall stinks. I think all of them need the bathroom. I don't want to see you like that at Christmas with your head glued to your chest. That's why I brought the book.

It was hard to find. When you sometimes remembered me, you told me to look for it. Now when I tell you I'm Lessy, you say, "Ah, Lessy," but I don't think you remember me at all, and a minute later you ask who I am.

The TV is on in your room. You're not looking at it. You're not looking at anything, like a dull curtain was pulled across your eyes. I say hi, and you look up with the sweetest smile and call me Paula. You think you're a little girl again, playing with your sister. I feel like running from the room and crying, but I don't. I want my grandma back. That's why I brought the book.

I wheel you out to the brick patio where the roses droop and sit next to you at a bench, and pull your shawl higher on your knees. We're alone. No one sees what we do.

"Look, Grandma," I say, showing you the book. "I found it."

A spark comes into your eyes. Then it's gone.

I open the book. It was hard to find. At first, I thought it was buried in the garden. I dug lots of holes and everyone got mad. I got a step stool and looked in the closets. I climbed up a stepladder and looked on the big shelf over the cars in the garage. Besides a bunch of dusty stuff I only saw spider webs and a mouse. I looked behind the washer and dryer and in all the cupboards. After a long time I found it in the attic. It wasn't easy. It wasn't in any of the boxes of old clothes and other books. I looked at each one, but it wasn't this one. This one you said was thicker than a loaf of bread is tall, and wider than my school binder. Then I remembered the rhyme you taught me. You told me to say it over and over again and never forget it. You said I'd need it someday. That's when I figured it out. *You* hid the book so no one would see it.

Now you're calling me Angie like I'm mother and you look cross. Don't you remember playing Go Fish, hide-and-go-seek, baking cookies, and beading and sand castles and picking blackberries in the summer and treasure hunts? Don't you remember we made dolls and you made it open its eyes and talk—not with your voice—with its own voice, like a fairy? Don't you remember when we played dress-up and I put on your ring and turned into a princess and we walked in a castle garden, far away? Don't you remember you read me fairy tales, and I told you I wished I had a fairy godmother, and you told me I did? You said you helped people. You said you'd done it when Grandpa was a baby, when his grandpa was a baby.

I have one more wish, Grandma. Can you guess it?

I turn the pages of the book, pointing to the pictures and letters you call runes. Is that it, Grandma? The one we need? You mutter things I don't understand. You clench your fist and keep saying, "Tangles, tangles, tangles." But your gray eyes are bright and looking at me now.

I'm pointing to words framed in a pretty drawing. I sing them softly, but you're shaking your head, saying, No, no, no. I'm chanting from another page. If we find the spell, you can leave, and I won't be alone.

Try, Grandma, try! Take me once more to the land where frogs are princes and swans princesses, where the lilies and bluebells sing and the feather of a bird is magic. Take me to your home in the clouds, your home in the sea, your home in secret groves. Help me find the trail of breadcrumbs so we can fly like birds to the land of time, where clocks run backwards and a fading rose buds anew.

Your eyes flash, hard like diamonds, hot like fire. You take the book from my hands. The pages whisper beneath your fingers. Part of one crumbles and blows away like pieces of an old leaf. Careful, Grandma, we might need that one!

You shake your head. "Tangles, tangles."

Find it, Grandma.

We turn the page. Where did the words go? I only see bits of them. The rest have faded. All that's left are brambles with thorns, drawn around the sides of the paper.

You tap the page hard. "Tangles, tangles."

I know, Grandma. They look like blackberry vines. We made blackberry nectar, remember? And you put a powder in it so the thorns would never stick me.

A tear rolls down your cheek. You stroke my face. "Lessy."

Yes, yes! What are the words? Tell me quick before you

forget. You bring my ear to your lips. "Say it, Lessy, the one I told you never to forget. Say it, say it—" You push me away. "Angie." Your face turns red. You're calling an aide who's walking by. You want to go back inside. I take your hands. "No, Grandma. I'm Lessy, Lessy! I promised. I didn't forget."

I glance at the aide. He didn't hear. I hold on to your hands. You try to pull them away but I won't let you go.

"Under twinkling stars at night," I begin. "Say it, Grandma, say the rest. You're the only one who can say it."

You look at me and say my name. You squint, your eyes holding mine.

"Under twinkling stars …" you say.

Yes, yes, Grandma. You know the rest. It's in there. I know it is. Find it, find it.

"Under twinkling stars …" you begin again. Light comes into your eyes. "—at night. I will hold you very tight. In the early morning sun, tangles, tangles, come undone."

I throw my arms around you. You hold me tight, just like in the rhyme. You rock me. I'm crying, but it's happy crying.

"Come, Lessy," you say in the old voice, the good strong voice that was always there for me. You stand on sturdy legs and take my hand. We look to the sky and spread fairy wings. Up we go, to the clouds, to the sea, to the secret groves. Can you hear them, Grandma? The lilies and bluebells are singing.

TITANIA

*S*he used to be famous; now she was invisible. After the accident, it needed to be that way. For someone with her talent it wasn't hard to do. All she needed was to sink into a role of anonymity, unnoticed, inconsequential, though on hot nights—it seemed they were almost always hot —she prowled the streets, a hood pulled low over her head, and then she was a shadow.

While she could move about unseen, she did so as little as possible. She holed up in her house, an unremarkable addition to millions of false, glittering lights. Groceries were delivered to her doorstep. The back bathroom remained unrepaired, as would the roof if it had leaked. She existed, caring for nothing and no one, and her dominion had shrunk to a speck.

All this changed with the nocturnal knock. Soft but firm, it invited curiosity. It drew her to the door, where she observed a man squinting up at the fisheye lens she was peering through. She read people with the practiced eye of her craft. Clothing, tension at the corners of the lips, gait, posture— these she construed like a well-schooled detective. This man eluded her. He was short and held a hatbox in one plump hand. An affable smile spread across his face and the flash of stars in his eyes was disarming. Unless he was a consummate actor, he appeared harmless.

The ensuing conversation left her excited, angry, intrigued. He wasn't selling solar panels, home-delivered meat, or a blessed afterlife. He was offering her a part in a play.

She unbolted and opened the door as far as the security chain allowed, keeping the right side of her face hidden. He seemed to look not at her but through the door at the foyer wall beyond, where photographs from productions of *Macbeth, As You Like It,* and *The Merchant of Venice* were hung beside rave reviews from theater critics, framed under glass and yellowed with years.

"The role of a lifetime," he said.

Excitement pulsed in her veins. Doubt followed on its heels. She hadn't set foot onstage for ten years. Not since the accident. Who could she play? A freak? A monster? "What role?"

"Titania."

She laughed bitterly and reappraised him. His brow was raised in hopeful expectation. No irony curled his lips. No vicious jest flashed in his eyes. But a crazy fan was not out of the question. He wouldn't be the first to discover her hideaway.

"Go," she said, making no attempt to temper the frost in her voice, "or I'll call the police."

"Hear me out," he replied.

He mocks me, she thought, and it was well that all the mirrors in the house had been removed, or the hardwood floors would have been littered with shards. As it was, she thought of opening the door wide, so he could see whom he would cast as Shakespeare's fairy queen, so he could see the ruined nerves and melted flesh the flaming car had bequeathed her.

"You could do it," he said, making no move to leave. He peered again in the direction of the photos and reviews. "They aren't wrong, you know. You're transcendent when you act. *You* disappear."

"I think you'd better leave."

She shut the door and latched it, but he called out. "I'll just leave this." He put the box on her doorstep. "Think of it as a prop, to help you get into the part. Directions and map are inside."

That might have been the end of it. On her next journey she would toss the unopened box into a dumpster. But after he'd departed she heard the distinct call of a varied thrush. A moment later it landed on the box and gazed up at the fish-eye. She didn't believe in totems, but if she had one, it would be this bird. Shy, secretive, seldom seen even in their forest habitat, the likelihood of finding one in the city was nil.

She quickly retrieved the box. Inside, door relocked, she opened the box and let out a short laugh. It was Titania's crown—a circlet of papier-mâché twigs and silk leaves, with a sparkling piece of green costume jewelry attached to the front. Tiny Christmas lights had been woven through the branches. A small battery pack was hidden in the back. It looked cheap, but under stage lights it would be otherworldly.

Despite herself, she put it on, half wishing she'd retained one mirror. But she didn't need it. She closed her eyes. The feel of it, the cool breath of it made the blistering summer night fade. For a moment, Titania sprang to life, just as she would portray her on stage.

She wavered. Calling beyond the door, the thrush decided it. An hour later she slipped into her car and headed out of the city. The directions and map were on the seat beside her, along with a brief note from him. It all seemed wild and improbable. But she drove east, and the glow of the city faded behind her. The stars seemed unusually bright. The moon loomed impossibly large against the silhouette of the mountains.

The stillness of the desert calmed the doubt and turmoil boiling inside her. Who was the director? Where was the theater? Who were the other actors? Did she know them? His note said, "They're masters of their craft. You belong with them. They need you. They lost their Titania."

A turn never appeared, and now she was several miles past the point indicated on the map. Had she missed it?

She doubled back and turned onto an almost invisible byway. She would have missed it but for the thrush, which swept by her windshield and alighted on top of a stop sign. The road began to climb. Soon she was winding up a mountain. The fuel needle tipped dangerously toward empty. Was there a gas leak? She calculated the distance to a gas station she'd seen. She wouldn't make it. Did it matter? Better to be lost out here than in the crowded world of concrete and tinsel.

She considered her role. Titania's conniving husband casts a spell over her so she falls in love with Bottom, a common weaver given the head of a donkey. Titania needed something new. Rather than the tricked queen, she could portray a powerful earth spirit.

If not for the thrush darting by, she would have missed the next turnoff. It was so shaded her headlights barely penetrated the gloom. The asphalt turned to gravel, gravel gave way to dirt, and the road inclined gently downward. The engine sputtered, coughed, and died, and the car rolled on momentum. Gradually it slowed and came to a stop before a gated fence. Ahead was a dark wood. Faint amber light glowed through the trees. Worst-case scenario, there was a cabin out here. Someone would help her refill her tank and get her back on the road to the city.

She removed the circlet from the box. Just looking at it bolstered her confidence. It's true—the right prop can do wonders. She set it on her head and sank into the role. In her mind, her hair was reddish gold, rather than mousy brown. Out of her car, she walked to the gate. A cool breath from the woodland caressed her face, a relief from the heat. The trail narrowed. As she went, the thrush flew ahead, singing. The shadows receded. Whispers, laughter, music strange and wonderful reached her ears. The actors, rehearsing nearby!

Will they accept me?

Funny to ask that. Not whether they'll like her portrayal, her command of the character—but will they accept her?

She thought of the man at her doorstep. He seemed different now, not of the city or even the world of actors. He belonged to something other—to the same world as the thrush, to the trees bowing toward her, to the humus cushioning her feet.

Light filtered down through the trees. She glanced at her watch. Two a.m. It couldn't be daylight. Stage lights? But soon the whole forest was bright. And cool and filled with ferns and spotted butterflies winging through the air like angels, and summer flowers, and everywhere was the scent of pines, and blue sky peeked through the cathedral dome of leaves.

Music floated toward her—a pipe, a drum, the stroke of a lyre. She came to an open glade. A stream tinkled like silver bells into a pool. She knelt at the edge and closed her eyes. She heard them all around, singing:

Titania!

Titania!

Startled, she opened her eyes and gasped. Reflected in the forest pool, Titania gazed at her in wonder. Her tresses billowed, as if floating on gentle currents. Leaves of gold and green, and berries of silver and white adorned her crown. Smooth, soft, unblemished, her face shone and glistened in the azure water. The play was almost forgotten. The memory of how she got there was a trembling leaf about to drop. She held on to it a moment, inhaling, breathing in the exquisite mystery of it. The next moment it would be gone, as in a dream.

The beat of their wings, the beat of their hearts, surged with hers. She turned to greet them, murmuring words wholly her own that rose from a subterranean source:

> *Come, my lord, and in our flight,*
> *Tell me how it came this night*
> *That I sleeping here*
> *was found.*[1]

---

1. From Act IV, Scene 1, *A Midsummer Night's Dream*

BLAZE

*U*ntil the cat came I lived a marginal existence. In 1689 such circumstances were not unusual for a child of uncertain origins, especially when that child is thrown on the mercy of a cold and mercurial lord. I was neither a member of the Earl's household nor a stranger. I was neither formerly a servant nor without responsibilities. My chief job was to care for his monstrous horse, Devil, largely because I was the only one the beast would allow near enough to curry, saddle, and feed. I wasn't paid for these activities, nor was I always required to attend to them. There were days when life was so dull, when so little was expected of me, that I took off for most of the day, exploring the surrounding woods and seashore.

It was on one of these sojourns that I caught my first glimpse of the cat. A storm had beaten down all morning but then passed, the last gasp of winter. I set off with no other aim than to wander through a fairyland of glistening fields and woods for a spell and then to park myself at the Earl's pond, hoping to pull out a fish or two to fill my stomach. I was just casting my line when the cat came shooting over a high rock overlooking the water and dived in. She was nothing more than a gray blur, leaving me doubtful as to what I'd seen. A dozen seconds passed and then she burst up, wet and bedraggled, a good-sized fish wriggling in her jaws.

She swam to the flat stones where I was perched and climbed on. After dropping the fish at my feet, she gave herself a good shake, spraying copiously, and stood staring up at me with eyes as blue and luminous as seashells. A bolt of black lightning shot from her forehead to the end of her nose, the only other color in her silver coat.

She pushed the fish to me, as if to share. She ate her portion raw while I cut off a piece and proceeded to roast it over a fire. After our meal, we lay on the rock and slept until the sun cast long shadows.

I took up my pole, tipped my hat at her, and began hiking home. To my surprise, she followed. "I've got no place to keep you and nothing to feed you," I said, pausing to run my fingers through her thick fur. It was the softest, most soothing thing I'd felt. She rubbed against my leg in reply. With a shrug I walked on while she trotted beside me.

A shortcut took me near the village. I had no mind to stop where I was assured of a fight with the local lads over the obscurity of my birth. Not that I was a coward. I generally came out the better from these scrapes, with bruised and swollen knuckles to show for it. But I had been away from my duties too long. Hurrying toward home—it hardly deserved to be called that—I heard someone call out to me. I turned back to see old woman Shaw, who sometimes pestered me for gossip about the Earl. Her nose was usually buried too deep in her cups to worry about. This time, however, she was sober enough to come weaving toward me.

"What've ye got their, Davie," she said, squinting at me with small bleary eyes and trying to see Blaze, as I'd come to call her, lurking behind my heels. All of a sudden she sucked in a breath and jerked back as though stung. "Keep away from her, Davie, she'll bring ruin!"

She staggered off faster than I'd ever seen her move. Blaze seemed sweet and innocent. Nothing but good had come since meeting her—first, the fullest meal I'd had in days, and second, the blessing of her softness. But this was Henwich, a village steeped in superstition. Ghosts appearing on Throcking Bridge, witches living in tree hollows where they cast enchantments, and spirits and demons haunting the woods where I'd fished were spoken of in guarded whispers in Wakeley Tavern. Old woman Shaw claimed she'd seen a selky, a creature of the sea capable of changing to a woman or whatever it desired on land, but returning to its real form, that of a seal, when it returned to water. Unlike most of the legends, she claimed selkies left no sealskin behind.

Her tongue was thick with spirits when she told the tale. I gave it no mind then and none now. Instead, as we strode down the road, I told Blaze about the Earl. "He's a moody man. He shuts himself up for days on end and speaks to no one. Often, the servants leave his food outside his door. Visitors are turned away, even the vicar, who stops by every fortnight, though he's generally chased off with curses. But then, after weeks of seclusion, something builds up inside the Earl like it's going to burst. That's when he wants his horse, Devil. They gallop full tilt across the moor and don't return until Devil's foaming at the mouth and near dropping." Blaze looked up at me as I spoke and sadness came into her eyes.

I had a bad feeling when Longmere came into view. The east tower was silhouetted against the sky, which the setting sun had ignited into an inferno. I quickened my steps and soon came upon a scene that almost had me turn tail and run. The Earl was pacing to and fro with that stiff limp before the barn, and cursing and slicing the air with his riding crop. Mrs. Geddes, the head housekeeper, was standing at a respectful distance, trying to calm and reassure him. He kept cutting her off, thundering at a volume that would have vied with the morning storm's explosions. One look at his riding outfit convinced me I was the cause of his wrath.

The groom, standing in a knot of onlookers, caught sight of me coming up the path. "There he is!" he called out.

Mrs. Geddes gathered her skirts and bustled toward me. "Where've you been? I oughtta box your ears. He's been in a rage for hours." She took a swing at me, but my battles with the village lads stood me well, and her fist swished by. Blaze bristled and hissed at the woman's attempt, which heartened me enough to face the Earl, even with the whip swinging in his hand. He'd threatened me with it before. By some providence, he'd never used it or laid a hand on me. I took this more as indifference than any softness or affection, for I'd never gotten that from him. Or anyone else.

He glared at me now. Wild tangles of shoulder-length hair framed his face, which was as inflamed as the sky. Escape was no longer an option. Though the manor staff had shrunk over the years, they'd formed a loose circle now and were of sufficient number to catch me.

"What are you waiting for?" the Earl yelled, at last. "Bring the horse!"

"Yes, sir," I cried, glad to be spared for the moment. I rushed to the barn. Devil nickered when he saw me and leaned down for me to stroke his nose. I stepped on a stool and threw a blanket onto his back. Because of his height and my age—I was just shy of nine years old—a contraption had been built to assist me. The groom already had the saddle in place. All I needed to do was slide it over until it rested on Devil. After that, cinching it up was easy.

He stamped his foot and snorted in that skittery way he had when he knew what was coming.

"Don't let him scare you," I said, stroking his neck to soothe him. "Just run like you always do and I'll give you this when you get back." I took a shiny red apple I always keep handy for him and held it up. He settled down enough for me to lead him to the Earl, who paced now like a caged tiger. When he saw us, he limped toward us.

Mrs. Geddes reached out as if to stop him, though she would never presume to hold him back. "Please, sir, it's late. What can you do now with the sun down?"

He stumped on, his eyes hot coals. Several of the men rushed to help him into the saddle. He shoved them away and growled that he wasn't a child. It took him several hops with his good leg in the stirrup for him to swing up. Mounted, he towered above us. The lines cutting his face deepened with fury, which turned on me. "I'll deal with you when I return." For the first time, he seemed to notice Blaze, who had followed me into the stable and back out, and who now regarded him from behind my heels with narrowed eyes. He pointed with the whip. "What's that?"

"She followed me, sir," I said.

"Followed you? From where?"

"From the pond."

He studied both of us a moment. "I want her gone when I return."

A great lump rose in my throat "Why?" I tried to keep the shrill desperation from my voice.

He pointed once more with the whip. "Gone." He spurred Devil, who charged across the sward with the fury of a demon, leaped a fence, and disappeared into the woods.

In a trice, Mrs. Geddes's stout form towered before me. "You heard him. Do it now so you're here when he gets back."

My lip trembled and I forced back tears. "But why? She hasn't done any harm."

"It's got the evil mark on it, sure as I'm standing. Get it out of here or you'll sink us all." She stalked off to the manse.

I sank to my knees, wrapped the cat in my arms, and cried into her softness. "I'm sorry, Blaze. You got to go away." She purred in reply, which made it harder to let her go, but at last

I set her down. "Come on, we'll go back to the woods. You can catch mice or go back to the pond. You're a fishing cat, though I never knew that was possible. You'll eat like a queen. I can tell you for a fact, the Earl won't give you anything."

I headed toward the woods but had to stop. Blaze was going the other way. "No—didn't you hear? I'll catch it good if you don't come." But she ignored me and trotted toward the house. I took off after her. Every time I sped up, she ran faster. When I slowed, she slowed. She passed the rose garden —an overgrown, ill-tended jumble of weeds—and headed up lichen-crusted steps to a side patio. She sprang onto the rim of a fountain. No water danced and splashed, and the stone spout had fallen and cracked long ago. When I joined her, both of us looked down into the lime- and moss-lined bowl.

"It must've made wonderful music," I said, reaching for her. She leaped away and slipped through the half-open door to the house. Inside, she'd stopped and waited for me. If I walked beside her, she allowed me to accompany her, even seemed to wish it, but if I reached for her, she ran ahead. She avoided the rooms where the household staff worked. There weren't many. In truth, most of the servants had quit because they weren't paid. Those who remained had been born on the property and had nowhere else to go. For the next hour we toured the house. Most of it was neglected and left to ruin. The water-stained walls, the broken balustrades, the cracked windows, the places where the roof leaked, all revealed how the Earl had let the once beautiful property deteriorate. This was most evident in the east tower, where most of one wall had crumbled away. Facing the sea, it was open to the elements, which lashed with wind and rain. This sad state of affairs could have been easily remedied. The Earl was not without resources—I'd often overheard Mrs. Geddes say he'd money aplenty. He simply forbade any of them to do the necessary repairs or upkeep.

Blaze had seen enough. With a sniff, she trotted outside, where she followed me readily enough. We cut through the far meadow to the edge of the woods.

"I'm sorry," I said, my heart heavy, for she was my first and only friend. "You can see how it is." She looked up at me with uncanny intelligence, gave what I took to be a feline shrug, and retreated into a tall patch of elderberry.

With sadness that left me hollow, I headed home, my steps unhurried, for my mind was laboring over all that had happened. The reaction of old woman Shaw was easy to dismiss as ravings. But Mrs. Geddes was a leveled-headed woman. Talk of evil and the devil never passed her lips. The Earl's reaction was even more mysterious. The estate had any number of cats roaming about the barn and fields. They were handy for keeping the mouse and rat population down. Why would he disapprove of this one? Whatever else might be said of the Earl, he feared no one. I could not believe he thought of Blaze as evil. Only one explanation remained. Her banishment was my punishment for not having his horse ready.

Fog was drifting in from the sea, punching holes in the glittering heavens, when Devil returned, sagging and foaming, the Earl slumped on his neck. I held out my hand to help him down. As usual, he refused, swinging off and stumbling on his game leg before he lurched off to the house without a word. I led Devil to the barn, where I wiped his glistening coat and fed and watered him. Then I crawled into the hayloft, my bed since arriving at the estate, and tossed and turned. Unable to sleep, I crawled to the wall to gaze at the manse between the slats. The windows were dark. Through the mist, it had the appearance of ancient ruins. I tried to imagine it as it had been, with candles blazing and laughter spilling into the garden on summer nights; children chasing puppies; neighbors stopping by and leaving with jars of honey or orange marmalade; women singing in the parlor to the strum of a lute; birds caroling in peach trees; and the lord of the manor spreading warmth and cheer across the shire. I tried to imagine what it would be like to live in such a place, to belong there, to be greeted with open arms and smiles. Instead of the dim and moldy hovels where the servants now lived, I saw a small room, freshly painted; a vase with fragrant roses on a desk where a lad such as myself might learn his letters and make something of himself; and a bed in a corner where each night he could lay his head and know he was home. I flung myself back on the hay and wept myself to sleep.

Next morning, when I showed up at the kitchen, the cook looked at me narrowly. "Did you get rid of it?" she asked, handing me a bowl of porridge.

"Get rid of what?" I replied, tucking into my meal. I couldn't recall if she'd witnessed last night's encounter with the Earl.

She rapped me on the head with knuckles as large and hard as almonds. "The cat, the cat."

"Yes."

"You better have."

"What's the devil's sign?"

"You saw it. Black lightning cutting its face. Did you wring its neck?"

I didn't get a chance to answer. Mrs. Geddes burst into the room.

"What kind of game are you playing?" she shouted, and swooped down on me like a harpy. With my ear pinched between her fingers, she towed me to the library. Blaze sat on the Earl's reading chair, licking her paw. The Earl stood regarding her, his face tight with annoyance.

"Remove it," he said, coldly.

Mrs. Geddes pushed me toward Blaze as though she were loath to touch her. "He'll get rid of it, sir, or I'll take it out of his hide."

The Earl dismissed us both with an indifferent wave of his hand.

I took Blaze deep into the woods. She strolled beside me while I pondered what it meant that she'd parked herself on his chair. Why hadn't she come to the barn? I could've kept her hidden there. Now I couldn't risk it. Because of her, the Earl had been inconvenienced twice, and Mrs. Geddes blamed me.

Back at the pond, I squatted and scratched her behind the ears. "This is where you live now. You can't go back there, you can't go anywhere near there. I'll get into a lot of trouble if you do."

She stared at me seriously, her luminous eyes flashing and shifting like opals.

"Goodbye, Blaze. I love you."

With a flick of her tail, she disappeared into the foliage.

Next afternoon, I was prowling the neglected halls of the house when I almost ran into the Earl, walking like a specter. He stopped dead in his tracks, stared at me a moment, and then continued on his way without a word. I looked after him. He was tall, with a broad frame. Not many years ago he'd been considered robust and handsome. Now he was rail-thin and painful to look at, and his haunted eyes receded as if they would withdraw from the world.

I can't say what prompted me, but I followed at a safe distance. When he reached the crumbled east tower he froze in his tracks. Blaze sat three yards dead ahead, gazing at him. He reached for a bell—the only functional thing in the room, the curtains tattered and mildewed long ago—and rang for Mrs. Geddes, who soon scurried up.

"Why is that here?" he asked.

Mrs. Geddes wrung her hands. "Davie took it away, sir. I watched him myself. He was alone when he returned."

"Get rid of it."

"Yes, sir." She grasped the cat by the scruff of the neck and stalked off, holding it like it was poison.

That evening, I was whittling by the barn when I overheard the Earl's manservant, Cooper, talking to the coachman.

"It was at dinner," Cooper said. "The thing came trottin' down the long table, passed the stuffed roasted pig, and sat before the Earl's plate."

"I heard his eyes smoked," said the coachman.

"Looked like he'd have a 'pleptic fit."

"What did he do?"

"Had Mrs. Geddes take it to a trough and drown it."

My heart sank. I ran to all the troughs, then checked the garbage heap and all around the property for newly turned soil where she might have been buried. I found nothing, though if I had, I don't know how it would have helped. A dark cloud hung over me when I returned to the barn. Imagine a cold, cold world, shrouded in darkness, without companionship or kindness. Now imagine that into this world a bright light shines. It illuminates every corner, obliterates every shadow, and suddenly the world is warm and beautiful and you have someone to share it with. It would be a wonderful kind of shock. Life, which formerly seemed barely tolerable, would ripple with excitement and possibility. Now imagine this miracle was suddenly snatched away, and you will understand what I was feeling as I threw myself into the hayloft and poured tears into the straw.

Mrs. Geddes, running into the stable like a frantic goose, interrupted my grief. "Davie, you in here? The master's calling for you."

Defiance rose within me. Why should I rush to do the bidding of the man who had snatched away happiness and broken my heart? Though I was hot with anger, a shred of sense remained in me. I climbed down the ladder and faced her.

"Come quick," she said. "The master's in a tizzy. I've

never seen him like this, swearing one minute he'll chase us all out and the next to hang us. His face goes white and red by turns and he keeps calling your name."

I folded my arms. "What does he want?"

"Come and see for yourself."

This was strange. The man could barely tolerate the sight of me. If he wasn't asking for Devil, what could he want? Intrigued, I set aside my bitterness, though I was prepared to tell him exactly what I thought of him if he said one unkind word to me, knowing I would have to leave Longmere forever and throw myself on the world.

When I entered his study, he was pacing before the fire. He turned when he saw me and pointed to his reading chair, the back of which was to me.

"You brought this into the house," he said. "You can get rid of it."

I had no idea what he could be talking about and I cared little. I was tired of being yelled at, neglected, ignored, and scapegoated. The look in his eyes stopped me short, a look of doubt, perhaps even fear—and this from a man who seemed to wish more for death than for life. Curious, I stepped around to see what all the fuss was about. With perfect ease and contentment, the cat sat happily washing her face.

"Blaze!" I cried, and running to her, swept her in my arms. She nuzzled my fingers and licked them and leaned forward to kiss my nose with her warm tongue. The light of a thousands suns streamed back into the world.

The Earl's voice cut in on my joy. "I want it out of here."

I whirled on him, Blaze cradled protectively in my arms. "Why? What did she ever do to you? She's the only good thing that ever happened to me. You're a mean old man and I hope you die."

Mrs. Geddes sucked in a breath. The Earl stared at me. To my surprise, he didn't grab the crop hanging on the wall or yell to have me thrown off the property. "Death would be a blessing," he said. "Maybe you could arrange a visit, as you have with the blasted cat. Take it away. Lock all the doors and windows."

I left with Blaze, not knowing where to take her. I had half a mind to start for the nearest seaport that night. But the road went through rough country. Highwaymen preyed on travelers, robbing them of money and jewels. A lad such as myself would either be killed or forced to join them. I had no desire to start that career at my age.

All I could think of was to take Blaze to the village. If I left her behind the butcher shop, perhaps the smell of fresh meat would be more inviting than the reception she was getting at Longmere.

What drew her to me, the manse, and most especially the Earl's chair was a mystery, but nothing save God could have stopped her from returning to us. Indeed, perhaps that was His intention. She was back at the manse before me. The Earl was beside himself. He personally oversaw her being sewn into a bag and thrown into an empty well. Next morning we found her curled up on a rug by the library fire.

Mrs. Geddes made the sign of the cross. "Pray, sir, pray. She's the devil's own."

The Earl made six more attempts, sending me to leave her miles away. Each morning, she greeted him punctually in the library.

"Don't mind him," I told her the last time as I carried her from the house. "He'll get used to you."

And so he did. Soon I found them in the library or at dinner, staring at each other, but the Earl ceased hostilities. He'd done much the same with me. Though I was too young to remember the first months, the story has been told to me often enough by different members of the household that I don't doubt it. Old woman Shaw showed up with me one day and demanded to see the Earl. She told him I'd been left on her doorstep as a baby. She'd felt compelled to care for me—I would have died otherwise—but now it was time for someone else to take the burden. Being lord of the shire, it fell to him. The Earl glowered and turned away, saying only that I was to be kept from his sight. He wanted no more to do with children than he did with the rest of the world.

I was relegated to the barn under the care of the groom, who had no interest in me other than to make sure I got up in the morning and did the work assigned me. At first the Earl scowled if we met by accident, but gradually he got used to me and moved on without comment. When I was big enough to saddle and care for his horse I took on the job, for while he had several fine and beautiful horses, he always chose Devil, who sent everyone running with his snapping and kicking— except me. I figured if I could work with him, perhaps I could find a place for myself. He was a giant among horses and fit for a god, with a splendid pelt that shone like ebony. He had thrown two of his prior owners, killing them. Despite warnings, the Earl bought him. It was whispered he had a death wish. Perhaps it was so. Devil threw him a dozen times before they came to an understanding. As for me, I'd found a place where I had some use.

No one knows for sure what made the Earl turn his back on the world. Some said a mad streak ran through the family. Some said it was disappointment in love. In Wakeley Tavern, where I sometimes escaped to learn something of the world, I heard the following story.

In his youth, the Earl was dashing and tall. His clean jaw and handsome features, not to mention his prosperous estate, made him the catch of three counties. When there was a ball, he was the centerpiece, admirers lining up to dance with him. When there was a contest, he was the champion. The other lads looked up to him, wanted to ride beside him, shoot beside him in a hunt, and the world was his oyster.

Then a girl like no other came to the shire. Her skin was as soft as rose petals; her hair wind-tossed and like spun amber.

Her smile was tender and her eyes!—blue-gray like the sea— gazed at the world with wonder. They captivated, mesmerized, and quickened the heart when she turned them on you. No one could stand before her and not feel it. She seemed to speak only what was noble and true, and she pierced the hearts of all who heard her.

She was a bright star compared to other young ladies who flitted about the Earl, tossing their curls and batting their eyelashes. While they were of noble birth, daughters of counts, earls, and even a duke, *she* had a nobility of a deeper, older lineage—a freshness, a spirit, a magic, like a sprite or a fairy from the old legends—and an ingenuousness that left all who met her breathless and enraptured. Even the other ladies —jealous and competitive for the Earl's attention—could not be angry or resentful around her. She breathed and pulsed and swelled with life.

Like everyone else, the young and vibrant Earl fell under her spell. The two of them were inseparable, seen at all the balls from shore to shore, and declared a handsome pairing. No one was certain of her background, though. Some said she was the daughter of a foreign prince, for she had an exotic air about her. Others said she hailed from Bavaria and was the daughter of a duke. Her answer when the Earl proposed to her only increased the rumors. She told him she loved him, would spend every moment of her life with him if she could. Alas, it was not meant to be. Her father would forbid the union.

The Earl had never met an obstacle he couldn't surmount. Now was no different. He proposed to meet her father, to show him the depth of his love and devotion to her. She said that was not possible. Her father would never see him, and she must go away.

"Where, where?" he cried.

She never answered, but told him that her father called and she must obey.

He swore he would not leave her side, he would follow her, he would proffer his suit. If her father saw the ardor of his love, he would not deny their happiness.

"He will never accept you," she said, "though it breaks my heart. I would rip it from my breast before I would hurt you, but he's a great and powerful lord and will not be denied."

"Then I shall take you where he can never find us. Come with me! We will sail to Istanbul, to Africa, to the New World. It doesn't matter where, as long as you're there."

The fire in his eyes set her heart beating wildly. There is no maiden who wouldn't have felt the heat of it, and it seemed she could see distant shores and climes. Caught up in the blaze of his thoughts, she imagined there might be a chance. They could slip away to a distant place where they could hide.

They left the next morning, letting the winds dictate where they might go. Where didn't matter. They were together, and for a brief time love wrapped them in a bubble, though to them, it was a flowering garden alive with birdsong.

Five days at sea, it burst. Dark and foreboding clouds lined the horizon. A sharp wind snapped the sheets, and the seamen looked nervously at the swells hurtling toward them.

She clutched his sleeve. "We must turn back," she said. "My father is angry."

"Never," he cried. "Who is he to deny me happiness?"

She looked at him piteously. "He's a great and terrible lord. To bring me back he will make the clouds black, the rain lash, the oceans rise into mountains."

The Earl laughed, half crazed. "Let him try! I spit in his face. He must be a hateful man to deny you happiness."

But a storm did come, like none seen since Noah. The boat swayed and tossed like a bit of wood. The waves swept half the crew overboard. The captain and first mate battled the wheel. The sails tore like paper. Fright gripped him at last, not for himself but because his arrogance might bring harm to her.

They had one chance, she said. He must lash himself to the mast. If his love was strong enough she could stay with him. Only then would her father relent. He tied himself to the mast. He laughed into the wind. He welcomed the rain beating down like a scourge. They couldn't dim the ardor of his love.

From time to time, he called out above the howling gale, "Art thou with me, love?"

And he would feel her touch on his hands and hear her voice near his ear. "I'm here, I'm here. Prove your love is stronger than his."

"I'll prove it," he cried. "I'll prove it, and then he'll bow down to me. Is he a god, that he can command our happiness? I won't be denied!"

Almost in reply, the storm doubled. The ship was spun like a toy. It was lifted high and dashed down, and water giants pounded the deck. At times it seemed they were submerged, that the ship was being pulled to the deeps, but then it rose again, only to be slammed and deluged once more.

Again and again, he called to her. She answered, she answered, and then he heard her no more. The mast splintered. With a terrible explosion it came tumbling down. The crossbeam fell on his leg. For a brief moment the world exploded into a thousand hot sparks, and then he passed out.

When he wakened, the storm had passed. The sea was glass, the sky clear. Birds winged above, crying. He tried to rise, looking left and right for her. He grabbed the sailors who were trying to put the ship into some kind of working order. Where was she? Had they seen her? No one had. She was gone. The sea had taken her. From that moment, he cursed earth, sky, and sea. He turned in on himself and his back on his fellow man.

I like to think the story is true. It lets me see him in another light and to expect nothing from him. I gave Blaze the same advice and it worked. After the Earl allowed her to coexist with him, she seemed to understand that his chair was off-limits. At night, she curled up on the bear rug before the fire. That is not to say that the Earl did not voice strong and hearty complaints peppered with oaths and blasphemies. He glared and growled at her like an enraged beast, while she gazed back, unruffled, and at times, it seemed, amused.

The flowers of spring wilted as summer came on. The first sign that anything was amiss was when he stopped riding Devil. After what happened the day I met Blaze, I had his horse saddled and ready in the mornings. It wasn't uncommon for a day or two to go by without him going out on the moor. But a week went by, and then another. The servants whispered among themselves. What they thought they didn't share with me, but I wondered what I should do about Devil. He stamped his foot and snorted with restless agitation. I began to understand the relationship between the two of them. The long rides helped both of them let loose pent-up fury.

While I was frightened of not having the horse ready, it upset Devil if he wasn't used. I could see the anticipation twitching in his ears, his nostrils flaring to blow out fire. Each day I unsaddled him, I never saw a sadder beast. At last, I could take it no more and went to Mrs. Geddes.

"What should I do about Devil?" I asked her.

She studied me a long moment. "Keep doing what you're doing." Weariness and sadness played around the edges of her eyes, alerting me to a change in things.

"He's not going to ride again, is he?"

"No, Davie, his riding days are over."

"Why?"

"It's not for you to ask or for me to answer." Without another word, she strode away.

By autumn, I figured it out for myself. The Earl was dying. A few weeks after he stopped riding, he stopped walking in the garden. He spent most of the day in his big chair, reading, sleeping, staring out the window, or sullenly regarding the cat. A few weeks more and he needed to be walked to his chair. When he could no longer reach the chair on his own shuffling feet, he screamed and cursed when a servant tried to carry him, and thereafter he stayed in his bed. Soon he couldn't lift his hand to eat. I know, because he asked me to be the one to feed him. Why he wanted me I can't say, unless he found it easier to take this indignity from a boy rather than from Mrs. Geddes or one of the men. He kept me nearby for anything he might need, and a cot was set up in a corner of his room.

Shortly after he took to his bed, the cat joined us. She liked to lie in the sun streaming through one of the windows or stayed with me on the cot. Most of the time, though, she parked herself on the Earl's chest, gazing at him. The first time this happened he turned red and I thought he'd unleash a torrent of oaths. Instead, he glared at her in sulky silence. Mrs. Geddes snatched her by the scruff of the neck, stalked to the window, and threw her out. Then she stomped over to me and raised her hand to box my ears.

To my surprise, the Earl interceded. "Leave him be."

"But surely, your lordship—"

"I said leave him be. The cat too."

Mrs. Geddes's brow narrowed with confusion, but with a curtsy, she left the room. A moment later, Blaze jumped through the window and resumed her face-to-face vigil on the master's chest. "Come to watch me die?" he asked, glaring at her. "Come to usher me to hell?"

Mrs. Geddes pounced on me almost the moment I was out the door. "What are you doing?" she barked, hand raised. "Trying to hasten his death?"

"It's what he wants," I replied, ready to dodge her blow.

"You'll hurry him to the grave. Is that what you want? What do you think will happen to you, what do you think will happen to any of us when he dies? He has no heirs. Longmere will be sold. We'll all be turned out."

I plucked up my courage. "He wants Blaze, and if you hit me or make me take her away, I'll tell him, I'll tell him right now." I started for the door.

"Now, Davie," she replied in a more conciliatory tone. "Don't be hasty. I was just thinking about your future. There's a good lad. Run along. I'll see that he's cared for."

I looked her in the eye. "If Blaze is gone when I come back, you'll have hell to pay."

Where I got the strength to face her down, I'll never know. She went livid for a moment, and then sighed. "It's what he wants, Lord knows why."

But I knew. Blaze's presence was a kind of penance. This was borne out when the vicar came to visit. At first the Earl refused him entry to the bedroom. But the vicar was not to be deterred and arrived one day while he slept. When the Earl opened his eyes, he scowled. "Begone! I won't suffer the sight of thee."

"We should pray, your lordship, pray for your salvation," the vicar replied.

"What good are your prayers? What good is your God to me?"

The vicar blanched. "You can't mean that."

"Mean it? I'll show you I mean it!" The Earl roused from his pillow and threw a vase of flowers at the vicar, who made a speedy exit.

For several minutes he strained and sucked for air. I offered him water, but he gripped my wrist with surprising strength for one so ill. "Life plays cruel tricks, Davie, showing you heaven and then snatching it away."

Tears misted my eyes. "I know," I said. For the first, perhaps the only time, understanding passed between us.

At times he drifted into delirium, talking to himself or yelling out in his sleep, "I killed her, I killed her, fie on heaven and earth, I killed her!" All the while, Blaze never left him. Once, near what seemed like it might be the end, when his breathing came in short, jerking motion, he wakened to find Blaze lying in her usual spot on his chest, her paw stretched out to him. "Do it!" he snarled. "Slice my throat with that devil claw of yours. Bring an end to it."

Blaze's eyes settled at half mast and she curled her paw the way cats do when they're happy to see you. It seemed awful to have her on his chest when he struggled to breathe. Again and again, I asked him if he wanted me to move her, and when he slept, I battled with myself over whether I should defy him and take her on my lap. But he forbade me to take her away when he was awake, and I couldn't go against his wishes when he wasn't.

Blaze decided it, sometimes curling by his feet, sometimes going out the window for water or food. She never spent much time satisfying either. She came back a short time later and resumed her vigil.

I kept my own breaks as short. I can't say why. I'd never been treated well, never felt affection for the man who had cursed and rejected me. Something compelled me to be with him now. It was a kind of challenge, to show him I was worth something, even if he didn't see it. Sometimes I thought he did, when I would waken stiff and sore in my chair to find him gazing at me. The look wasn't tender. But the hardness in his eyes might have softened a bit and the coldness had thawed.

One night, I wakened in my chair, sleep clinging to me like fog. For a moment, I felt sure I was dreaming. Instead of Blaze on the Earl's chest, I saw a woman sleeping by his side. Her hair tumbled like spun amber, her skin was as soft and smooth as young rose petals, even in the low candlelight. Her gown clung to her like thousands of tiny stars. The Earl's murmuring roused her. She lifted her head, revealing eyes the color of the sea, and so exotic as to have the look of another world about them. She regarded him with a tenderness I'd never seen on the face of another human being.

Startled, I sucked in a breath. I believe she was already aware of my presence, but now she glanced at me. Everything about her was wonderful and strange and a little frightening, so that I withdrew into the shadows. At once I had the sense that I was being allowed to view what was unfolding but that I should remain quiet and not interfere.

The Earl's eyes focused on her and flared. "What dream is this? What phantom? My mind plays tricks, punishing me even now? Shall I be haunted into the grave by you?"

"Hush … 'Tis no dream," she said. Her voice was as sweet as blossom honey, as enchanting as Orpheus's lyre. He tried to lift his head from the pillow. She pushed him back gently. "Shhh, don't tire yourself."

She knelt by his bedside and cradled both his hands in hers. They spoke in soft tones. He stared at her amazed and repeated, "You live, you live?" She smiled, looking at him with all the gentleness and love the heart is capable of.

Only a few words floated over to me. From her: *You must not blame … I should have told you … I was crazy with love and didn't think.* From him: *I thought you perished …*

At times I drifted off to sleep, only to waken again thinking it was the same dream, continuing. But then he asked her something that startled me to full attention. "The boy … is he mine?"

"Should it matter?" She scolded as gently as one might to a young pup.

What might have been comprehension and then self-reproach came into his eyes. He sighed. "No, but I'd like to know."

"No, Frederick, but you must—" She whispered the rest into his ear.

Later, she climbed back next to him, as if to keep him warm. Sometimes she sang, haunting melodies never heard by human ears. They were such as a bird might sing to its mate by moonlight.

Before dawn I fell asleep. The clattering of the breakfast tray wakened me. The woman was gone, the cat too. The Earl was sitting up in bed. His face glowed, suffused with warmth and color. From time to time, he turned his gaze on me. I can't say he'd softened, but he wasn't as hard either. Over the next days, his energy increased. He ate, he napped, he rose and asked me to walk him to the window. By the end of the week, he was up and in his chair. By two weeks he was taking meals in the dining room and sitting in the sun in the garden all afternoon.

There were other changes. As it became clear he would live, as he returned to his normal routine, he no longer wished me out of sight. It wasn't that we talked—we didn't. But I was moved in from the barn and given my own room. This wasn't a servant's chamber no bigger than a closet, but one of the large airy rooms on the second floor with a balcony and view of the gardens, fields, and verdant woods beyond. That's not all. I was expected to be in the dining room or the garden when he took his meals. I wasn't just there for company, and vigil was no longer needed, for day by day his illness was a thing of the past, receding the way a nightmare fades from memory until one but snatches at threads. No, there was a place setting for me. When the food tray was brought in, I received a serving of everything he ate. Imagine my amazement after years of eating scraps others left behind.

I can't say he was completely altered. Though we spoke little—and never about the cat or the mysterious woman—he seemed concerned that I was comfortable. I would even say he took pains to ensure that my old status was a thing of the past, and the servants treated me accordingly. He obtained a governess for my education and on cold or stormy days he heard me at my lessons, reading French poetry or a passage from Homer or Plato.

This transformation didn't stop with me. He kept Mrs. Geddes busy repairing and redecorating the manse, hauling down ripped and dingy curtains; putting up new and brightly colored ones; supervising the carpenters in the renovation of the south wing; restoring the fallen staircase; building a new wall in the east tower so the bitter wind no longer shrieked in from the sea. He hired new workers to keep the estate up. Weeds were pulled from the garden, dead plants removed and new roses, geraniums, and marigolds planted, so that spring brought color and songbirds roosted and sang. The fields were tilled. Soon crops were pushing green shoots up in long rows. The soil itself seemed different. Where before it had looked dead, dull, and impoverished, it was now dark and rich and there didn't seem to be anything that wouldn't grow in it.

As I grew older, he turned some of the responsibility for overseeing the repair and maintenance of the estate to me. I couldn't account for this in any way, for it seemed to me that surely there were others more qualified. But he periodically brought me into his study, showed me plans for this or that— a gazebo, a new well, piping, roofing, fencing, and the like— and handed them off for me to supervise. By the time I turned sixteen, I was running Longmere, not like a housekeeper, like a lord.

That year he suffered a stroke. Five days later he died. After the funeral, attended by myself, the servants, and a few villagers, his solicitor called me into the study to read his will.

The man squinted and scrutinized the document for several minutes, as if he could not be sure of what it said, though I knew for a fact he had written and notarized it himself, having seen him and the Earl preparing it not many weeks before he died.

"Do you know what's written here?" he began.

"The Earl never discussed it with me," I replied, trying to bolster my courage and keep the tremor from my voice. I had no idea what would become of me if the Earl had decided to sell the property and turn us all out. For all I knew, he might have a distant cousin somewhere whom the solicitor had found. If so, this place where I had resided, which I had tended and nurtured and grown to love, would no longer be my charge. I had thought this problem through, biting my nails down to the quick after the Earl's stroke, and had determined I would seek my fortune in London or perhaps take up on a trading vessel to see the world. It's a wide and dazzling place when you're sixteen, though I would leave with a heavy heart.

The solicitor took a deep breath. "My lord, he left it all to you."

I rocked on my feet and my head went light so that it felt as though I had grown as insubstantial as a down feather and was floating to the ceiling. I couldn't comprehend what he meant. What had been left to me? Some heirloom? Perhaps a cameo, a favorite book, his walking cane? I looked around the room, seeking the thing he had bestowed. Seeing nothing, I looked back at him. "I don't understand."

"He has transferred ownership of Longmere—its lands, its properties, all he owned—entirely to your name."

Still struggling to comprehend, I said, "But I have no name." I felt a chill go through me too, as who would accept the validity of an inheritance bestowed on a lad with no name.

"He took care of that. Two weeks ago, he gave you his name."

"Am I ... Am I his son?"

"He never said. He just insisted that the change be made and that it be something that could never be challenged, no matter who might lay claim on the estate."

I signed the necessary papers and walked him out. After

which I rambled far into the countryside, trying to fathom my sudden shift in fortune. My feet took me to his grave. I laid a few wildflowers I'd gathered on the freshly turned soil. From the corner of my eye, a motion by the headstone made me glance up. I found the cat sitting on top, regarding me. I have no doubt it was the same one that had plagued him and that had ushered in miracles and secrets. She had the same black bolt others had called the mark of the devil.

"Blaze!" I called out. I so wanted to take her up in my arms and sink my fingers into her fur and feel her nuzzling my nose. As I approached, she jumped from the stone and took off across the field. I followed, and when she got too far ahead she paused on a rock or tree stump and waited, but when I drew near, she took off again and then disappeared into the forest. I caught glimpses of her there—streaks of gray jumping through ivy. I saw her pass through the perimeter of the trees as they gave way to heather and led to a cliff. When I burst from the foliage, Blaze was nowhere to be seen. Little grows there and there was nowhere for her to go. Instead, stepping lightly up the trail leading to the cliff's edge, I saw the woman who had been by the Earl's bedside all those years ago. She glanced back at me with those eyes, more luminous than opals, and smiled. If she'd changed a day, I couldn't see it. Even her gown looked the same, light, airy, and sparkling.

When she reached the cliff she turned back for a moment, her wind-tossed hair rippling. Then she leaped.

I rushed forward, crying out in alarm. When I got to the edge I looked down, searching for her, hoping beyond hope she'd survived. All was foamy chaos crashing on the rocks. Then her head emerged. She gave one look at me and dived. As her body showed above the surface, a seal tail came with it, arcing out and back into the waves.

THE TEA PARTY

The invitations to the tea party smelled sour, like turned milk, and had the hint of something medicinal. The invitees, the three children of Sir Robert Wainwright, had received these invitations before. In the past, the two sons politely declined. "Too much work at the office, pop. Busy busy busy. You know how it is," the eldest, George, would say, dictating to his secretary. Jack, the younger son, would wire a quick note: "Hope to make the next one. I'm off to Africa. Will send postcards!" Cards never arrived. Over the years, the replies became increasingly terse. "Can't make it." "Maybe next time." "Wish I could. Sending up a ham instead." The old man laughed viciously when he got this note, tossed it into the fire, and gave the ham to one of the servants.

He never included an RSVP card and envelope in invitations to his third child, Clara. He didn't need to. She always arrived before the appointed hour.

What possessed the sons to attend this latest party is a mystery. Perhaps it was the tremulous writing in gold ink or the scent of sour milk. Perhaps they sensed that it was less invitation and more of a summons. Whatever the reason, they arrived on time, and a servant escorted them into the great hall. The curtains were pulled, blocking the afternoon sun. Dust had settled on the shelves and hardwood floor like a blanket of fine snow. The high, impersonal ceiling was lost in shadow. Sir Robert sat in a large, stiff-backed chair a few feet from the crackling flames on the hearth, a blanket over his knees. The heat penetrated the room only a few feet.

The boys gave Clara, seated with folded hands near the old man, a curt nod. It was Sir Robert that commanded their attention. His mass, which frightened them as children, had melted from his frame. The terror of their childhood, thus reduced, made the sons smile.

The old man smiled, too, without mirth. "So you've come."

"Sure, pop," George said, fiddling with the keys in his pocket. "Had a little opening in the schedule. You know how it is, business keeps you running."

"Yes," Sir Robert replied, still with that savage smile, "I know how it is." He turned to Jack, who had plunged recklessly through ruinous careers and investments. "And you, here for another, 'few pounds to get you by'?"

Jack glanced at his brother and shifted from foot to foot. "I've been looking at an Andean railway. The shares are cheap and ..." His father's cold level gaze muzzled him.

"I'll cut to the quick," Sir Robert said. "I'm dying. You'll want to know the terms of my will." He paused to gauge their reaction. They waited, George's jaw twitching, Jack leaning forward with unmasked expectation.

"I've given all of my assets to charity," the old man continued, "save what is in this house, and one thing of greater value than everything else combined." The boys glanced at each other questioningly, but he pointed a bony finger at them. "You know nothing of it, but it is hidden somewhere on the property and goes to whoever finds it before sundown."

He rang a bell. A servant entered with a tea service and

put it on a table beside the old man. He waved a hand toward an eight-cup teapot, always an eight-cup, as if the whole brew would ever be needed. "I don't suppose you'll stay for tea?" he asked, and that brutal smile creased his lips.

His sons were already backing away with little bows and apologies. When they were halfway from the room, they turned and scampered out like two dogs in search of a bone.

He picked up the teapot with a wavering hand.

Clara pulled her chair closer. "Let me, father." She opened the lid on the tea box and sniffed the contents. "Assam and...?"

A very different smile spread across his face—soft, tender —and the years seemed to melt away. He nodded toward a window, which overlooked the garden. "Something special for today. Linden blossoms. Buds from the top of the tree."

"Shall we have the party beside it, where it's warm?"

"A cup here first. I'm cold ... so cold ..."

She gazed in the direction the boys had departed. "They don't mean anything by it."

"They mean it."

She measured eight teaspoons into the pot and replaced the lid. While the tea steeped, she fixed him a plate of cucumber and goat cheese crumpets. As she handed it to him, crashing erupted upstairs. "They'll destroy the house." She began to rise.

"Let them." The hard smile returned. "You don't want it, anyway."

"No. I don't want it. I have everything I need."

They could hear furniture being dragged across the floor, drawers being pulled out and thrown aside. Something large and heavy fell and shattered.

She lurched to her feet. "They're breaking your vase."

"Yes," he said, looking at his withered hands. "Made from the wheel in the barn. With these fingers." Another pot crashed to the floor, and the crystal chandelier above Sir

Robert jingled from the vibration. "Pour," he said. "There's nothing up there I want. The only thing of value is here." He waved at the space between them and gazed longingly at the teapot.

She sank to her chair. "Where's the silver tea service?"

"Sold for charity. This one I kept hidden. I don't think you've seen it. Pour."

"It's beautiful ..." A painting on the teapot of the garden outside seemed to shimmer. This was how she would remember it, years hence, the spreading tree growing from a lush bed of turquoise and violet flowers, and the little brook bubbling nearby, dawn-touched and golden.

She poured. Steam rose and enveloped them in the bouquet of blossoms, memories of laughter and gifts, and perhaps a whiff of sweet times to come. Then everything faded but the sound of flowing tea. This too trailed away, merging with the murmur of the brook, coming like the echo of a dream from the painting on the pot. As she handed him a cup, they locked eyes.

"You heard it?" He leaned forward.

"I heard it."

He settled back into his chair. "I knew you would. Have I told about my time at the Barabar Caves?"

"Maybe not all the stories," she replied, for something new always did come out.

By the end of the first cup, he had moved from tales of the war to tales of his boyhood, skipping school, building forts, making knives out of nails flattened by passing trains.

"Let's go to the garden," she said, when the sandwiches had been eaten. A servant helped her move him into a wheelchair, and with the tea service on his knees, she wheeled him through the house. Books, paintings, and broken pottery lay scattered on the floor. Curtains had been ripped from the windows. Jackets, pants, and shoes littered the hallway. A horrific banging rattled the house, and soon they passed walls that had been torn open, no doubt by an axe.

She wheeled him out of the wrecked house into the sunlight and down a cobbled path, until they reached the linden tree.

She poured him another cup, and he asked, "Have I told you about the curious way I met your mother?"

She sipped her tea, relishing the warmth of the cup in her hand. "Tell me again. I want to remember everything."

He told how they met at a party in Bombay, how they journeyed through the Khyber Pass, and of their adventures from Australia to Singapore. The third cup of tea brought tales of his parents and their scandalous love, for he was a lord and she was a music hall singer.

Jack emerged from the mansion with a shovel. Soon, dirt and flowers were flying.

Clara started to rise. "This is too much. They'll ruin it all."

"It was ruined long ago." Bitterness lined Sir Robert's face, but it softened as he nodded toward the pot. "The last cup, for one last tale. One you haven't heard."

She poured, and as she handed him the cup, Jack stalked over to their corner of the garden, panting like a dog, his face and clothing streaked with grime. He lifted his spade to pierce a bed of daisies.

Sir Robert raised his hand and stopped him. "Tea, Jack?"

Jack glanced at the lowering sun and then took aim at the flowers with his spade.

The awful smile returned, twisting the old man's features. "There's nothing to find here. Dig elsewhere."

Jack marched off, overturning benches and flowerpots on his way, until he disappeared inside the garden house. Soon, the sound of ripping boards sent a flock of pigeons skyward.

"Pour," said Sir Robert. "One last story."

The tea was lukewarm now but still fragrant. They dipped

their little lemon cakes, savoring each bite, as Sir Robert began.

"One night, before you were born, a terrible storm struck. The wind screamed through the trees. Rain lashed the windows all day. Despite the lightning and thunder, we fell asleep that night, but hammering on the door roused us. A coachman cried out that his carriage had overturned, its occupant hurt. We gathered the servants and carried the injured man inside. No bones were broken, but his back had seized up, and he couldn't walk. The storm passed, and over the next days, he was able to sit in this garden—under this very tree—and shared tea with me. He told me he was a painter, and asked if I would let him stay to sketch and paint. I told him that my house, gardens, and fields were his. He lingered many weeks and returned from London often, well into the spring. Sometimes he would come and watch me throw pots, but most of the day he was out, drinking the air, as he called it, and the light. At night, we smoked cigars, drank brandy, and played chess, but he was always up early, hauling his easel from one corner of the estate to the other."

Sir Robert looked around the garden. "But this was his favorite spot."

The sky was turning violet. He put down his cup and watched Jack and George trudge up the path of trampled flowers toward them.

"Well, you've had your fun, old man," Jack said. "If there's a treasure, it's not on the property."

George glared down at the old man. "It's not sensible. You must have a will."

Sir Robert drew an envelope from his coat pocket. "I have. Right here." He pointed a bony finger at the boys. "All that you've ruined, the house, the lands, go to the two of you. You'll fight over it like rabid dogs for years, though it's written in ironclad ink by my solicitor. Clara gets this tea service."

Jack leaned forward, his eyes eager. "What about the silver one?"

"Too late for that, Jack. It's sold."

George snarled, "Well, sis, see what your wasted hours on him got you. One of his bloomin' pots."

Sir Robert laughed. "He doesn't get it, does he Clara?"

She shook her head. "No, he doesn't get it."

"You understand. I know you understand."

"Yes, father. I understand." Clara picked up the teapot. Her finger brushed the painted tree, spreading like the linden tree above her. She turned the pot over, and read the inscription:

For my friend, RW, for sharing tea.
Claude Monet.

THE MASK

*J*essica Lansing would laugh if she were told that metaphysical principles were real and had rules, that actions and reactions had a cosmic tally sheet, that small forces—originating, say, in a child—could destroy large forces as thoroughly as colliding matter and antimatter. Per Jessica, such things were palliatives for weak minds. Life was predictable if you worked hard, planned, and exerted your will.

Nowhere was her will exerted more than in the six-hundred-square-foot center of her universe, which she surveyed now with satisfaction and an eye to detail. Masks hung on a bulletin board, empty white shells to be painted and decorated. Below each mask, rectangles of construction paper bore the name of each student, printed in a child's hand with marker pen. Books sat straight on the shelves, encyclopedias stood in order like soldiers at attention, the ceiling was free of frivolous mobiles, and the walls were clear of distracting posters. Neat rows of desks. Chairs straight. Students seated with upright spines and folded hands. All eyes on her.

Shouting was unnecessary. She spoke in a quiet, measured

voice. "Children, you may stand and line up at the bulletin board in the order of your row."

The children stood. She noted how their eyes widened and darted from side to side, glancing at their neighbor to make sure they coordinated as instructed. Good. A little terror brings discipline to young minds and opens them to learning. Parents and teachers were far too lax, and children showed no respect for their elders. Well, the grownups only had themselves to blame.

An experienced teacher knows every motion, every sound in the classroom. There were no whispers in *her* class, but if there were, she would know the offender. Listening out of turn was just as bad as speaking out of turn, and both students would be dealt with. Thus, there were no whisperers. Or liars, cheaters, spit-wadders, or paper airplaners. Only studious little minds.

As the children began to file from their seats row by row, Miss Lansing heard the distinctive roll-tap-tap-roll of a pencil traveling across a desk and then landing on the tile floor. The pencil's owner bent, snatched up the offending object, and stuck it in her desk. Though she had paused only for a moment, she lost her place in line, and had to squeeze between two students from another row.

"Emily," Miss Lansing said, in that quiet voice, but now with an edge of firmness.

The girl looked up at her with the eyes of a frightened doe.

"Why are you out of order?" Miss Lansing asked.

The girl froze. "My pencil dropped," she said at last, her voice a hoarse whisper.

"What did I tell you?"

Emily stared up at Miss Lansing as if she had been asked to solve a complicated algebra operation. "To keep my pencil in my desk?" she ventured.

"Then why didn't you?"

This question might as well have been calculus. Emily looked desperately to her classmates for the solution.

"Answer me." The muscles between Miss Lansing's eyes contracted. She had practiced the look in the mirror and knew that two thin lines formed above the bridge of her nose. Corporal punishment was unnecessary. These lines turned on this girl were enough to quell the class for days.

"I don't know, ma'am."

"I'll tell you why. Because you weren't thinking. In this class you will think. And you will learn. Go find your place in line."

Emily scurried to her place in the queue. On command, the children took their masks and returned to their desks.

Mask making was not Miss Lansing's idea of a proper education. It stimulated the primitive part of a developing brain. Allowing the imagination to roam is like letting a wild mustang loose. But the school board was visiting next week to select a model classroom and nominee for teacher of the year. They expected art in the curriculum. Jessica Lansing knew how to play the game. And win. The same way she'd won first prize for the sixth-grade science fair when she was eleven. The way she'd been elected to student body president in high school, won a President's Education Award, and received a Barry M. Goldwater Scholarship for mathematics. Besides, the teacher of the year would win a three-month traveling sabbatical, attending educational conferences and meeting with teachers and principals across the country. She didn't care the smallest fraction for the conferences or meeting other educators. The fools had nothing to offer but dangerous ideas. But the conference schedule included, among other choice spots, a stop at the Disney Grand Floridian Resort and Spa, in Orlando. Jessica Lansing had never been to Orlando, and after all her hard work over the years and slavish dedication to the little cretins in her classroom (monsters was a better word), sipping champagne while she soaked in a whirlpool in a world-class hotel was long overdue. Losing was not an option.

The classroom door opened. The principal, Mr. Jeffries, and a small boy stood in the doorway.

Mr. Jeffries wore khaki pants and a short-sleeved shirt, the kind of casual attire that leads to lax minds and erodes discipline. "Children," he said with a smile, "we have a new student today. Please welcome Christopher."

The boy gazed at the other students, around the classroom, and then fixed his attention on Miss Lansing. His eyes were wide open and black like a beetle's. If he blinked, she couldn't see it.

"Thank you, Mr. Jeffries," she said, with an expression, also rehearsed before a mirror, that conveyed kindness, caring, and amiability. "We'll make Christopher feel right at home. Won't we, class?"

The class, sitting with folded hands and stiff smiles, intoned in unison, "Yes, Miss Lansing."

Mr. Jeffries brought laced fingers to his chest and gave a little passionate shake. "I knew you would."

When he left, Miss Lansing's face hardened, and she turned a disapproving eye on Christopher. He was small for a fourth grader. His jeans were faded, worn, and frayed at the cuffs. And though they were clean, they bore evidence of grass and dirt stains. A small hole had opened up at one knee. His hair flopped every which way and was cut unevenly.

"There are three rules in this classroom, Christopher," she said. "Don't talk unless you are called on. Don't get out of your seat unless you are told to. And eyes on me when I'm talking. In other words: obey, obey, obey."

He stared up at her with those unblinking beetle eyes. This was unprecedented and bordered on defiance. He should have been squirming by now like a worm on a hook.

"The punishment for breaking the rules is Super Glue. Do you know why?" she asked.

He waited, gazing silently up at her.

"Christopher, I asked you a question. Do you know why?"

His voice came soft and sibilant. "Why would I know? I just got here."

Miss Lansing gave an indulgent laugh to save face before the class, whose mouths were beginning to fall open. "You will learn, young man, that a smart tongue gets you nowhere in this class. Do you understand that?"

"Yes."

"Good. Then we're beginning to get along. You may take that open seat." She pointed to a desk in the back row. "You will learn soon enough about Super Glue if you break the rules."

When he was seated, she brought him an apron, scissors, prepared papier-mâché

strips, plastic bowl, and a mold for a mask.

"We're making self-portraits," she said.

The student on his right was told to bring him water from the sink and then to show him how to lay strips of papier-mâché onto the mold. After circling the classroom, to observe each student's project and to give assistance where needed, Miss Lansing returned to her desk, where she removed a brochure for the Disney Grand Floridian Resort Spa from one of the drawers. She inhaled deeply, almost smelling the scent from the flowers on the photo of page one. The Royale Package, 150 minutes of pure pleasure—lunch, facial, aromatherapy massage, and sugar exfoliation. That was the one she would sink into. And her travel per diem would cover the $430. Afterward, she would lounge at the pool, sip wine, and feast her eyes on beefy, Speedo-clad cabana boys ...

Her internal teacher's clock didn't allow her to fall too long into daydreams. It roused her, as it always did with bitter regularity, five minutes before the end of the period.

"Children," she said with a note of weariness—certain the

children would hear it as discontent with them, "begin cleaning up. I don't want to see a drop of paint."

The class screwed lids on tempura-paint jars, washed brushes in the sink, wiped up fallen drops of water and color, and were seated again on the double with folded hands, eyes on her. All except the new boy, who was still laying papier-mâché strips on his mold. He hadn't put on his apron. Streaks of floury paste ran up his arms and smudged his shirt and pants. His desk looked like it had been finger-painted with the stuff.

She was in front of him in a flash and asked in her coldest tone, also rehearsed, "Christopher, what did I tell you about listening to me?"

Christopher dipped a strip of paper and laid it on the mold. "To obey you."

"And what did I say?"

"To clean up and not leave a drop of paint."

Miss Lansing's jaw dropped. When she pressed her lips together at last her mouth throbbed with tension. The little imp hadn't been engrossed in his project. He was openly defying her. He would soon learn this was a game he couldn't win.

"Then why didn't you obey?" she asked, in her sharpest voice.

He dipped another strip of paper, and then held it over his water bowl, watching excess water drip off. "I want to finish this."

An urge welled in her to smash his mask with her fist. But that wouldn't do. The other children must not see her lose control. Her method was based on quiet tyranny and terror.

She glared down at him. "Do you remember the punishment for disobeying me?"

He laid the strip onto the mold and smoothed it down with his fingers. Then he gazed up at her, his lips curled in a whisper of a smile. "Super Glue."

"That's right," she replied, and pointed to a chair in a corner of the classroom. "You will spend recess there. If your bottom moves from that seat, I will glue it down with Super Glue."

Christopher held up his mask and pointed to the chin, where he hadn't put any strips. "I just need to finish this spot."

She was about to say, "I don't care, march over to that chair," when her gaze fell on the mask. The strips had been laid haphazardly. The layers buckled and bulged. When it dried, some of the paper would blister open. But what arrested her attention were the eyeholes. The shape was like the masks primitive tribes made to frighten enemies or ward off evil spirits—two slashes forming a sinister V.

Queasy coils twisted in her stomach. A teaspoon of her Jenny Craig Pasta Napolitana lunch (only 280 calories and 4.8 grams of fat) bubbled to her throat, scalding it.

The recess bell rang. For a moment, she heard it as a terrible clanging, as though a train hurtled through the middle of her head. Christopher began to rise.

She checked the urge to clutch her head and straightened her jacket, too experienced a teacher to be rattled by a clumsy student art. "Where are you going?" she asked, voice pitched low and cold. It restored her confidence.

"To the chair."

She pressed her index finger firmly on his desk. "Sit back down and finish the eyes."

"That's the way it goes."

"I don't care." *It's ghastly.* "I won't have this in my class-room. Fill them in up to here." She indicated the area of the mold where human eye sockets began. *Not these demon holes.*

Christopher stared up at her with those unblinking eyes. She couldn't read him, which made her want to wring his neck, but she gazed back at him until he began adding layers where she wanted them.

The rest of the day ran smoothly. They completed worksheets on subtracting fractions and spelling words with short "e" sounds. The masks were hanging on the wall again. Christopher's was the only one unpainted, but the eyeholes were on par with the other students', and that was all that mattered. The last thing she needed when the board toured her classroom was for them to see a bizarre hell-mask. The day ended serenely with silent reading of *Jason and the Argonauts*. While the children buried their noses in their books, she indulged in daydreams of walking barefoot on a moonlit Cocoa Beach—only an hour and nineteen minutes from the Grand Floridian Resort. It was all calculated. And Orlando boasted many ways for her to get away from the little gremlins visiting Disney World.

That night, she slipped into a hot bath of gardenia-scented bubbles—lord knows, she'd earned these little luxuries—and sipped a glass of Clos du Bois Chardonnay, a miracle purchase at $9.99. The tensions of the day melted away, and daydreams of Florida played across her mind. She was just drifting into sleep when she thought she heard drumming—deep, pulsing, primitive.

She sat up, but the sound stopped.

A hypnagogic hallucination, that's all. Her doctor had told her that's what they were, after she complained of several of them, wondering—with embarrassment and considerable anxiety—if she was developing an incipient psychosis. Just the brain beginning to dream, he'd told her, as it passes into sleep. Hypnopompic hallucinations, also normal, occur as a person transitions from sleep to being awake. She'd had a few of those, too. But both types had been visual. Never auditory. Never music. Never drums beating as if a tribe deep in a jungle were working themselves into a frenzy before an attack.

"Calm down," she muttered, poured herself another glass of Clos du Bois, and ran more hot water into the tub.

The second glass was the perfect soporific for a restful night's sleep. The next morning, she laughed the whole thing off. True, the little rascal Christopher had rattled her, but now she was prepared for him. If he doesn't blink, let him suffer with dry and dusty eyes. As for his behavior, she was Jessica Lansing, the terror of the fourth grade. There wasn't a child she couldn't control. Confidence restored, she strode into the classroom, sat at her desk, and removed a checklist from a drawer. The items were the icing on her plan to win Teacher of the Year, and she tapped each with satisfaction.

1. Flowers on her desk, to convey nurturance and sensitivity. Check.
2. Children's desks neat, organized, and in straight rows and columns. Check.
3. Majority of the class exceeding math standards. Check. (The children's STAR test scores were on file and would be known to the board. Perhaps she would cap it off with a little oral demonstration. When the committee entered her room, she might call on two students who had mastered sixth-grade operations.)
4. Order and put up goals poster, to inspire young minds. Ordered.
5. Order and put up values poster, to foster good citizenship. Ordered.
6. Tear down both posters after review committee tour. To be done.
7. A reminder on the whiteboard of state report due dates. Check.
8. Speak at the PTA on importance of nightly reading. Check.
9. Endorsement letters from colleagues. Check.
10. Masks completed and displayed, to show cultivation of artistic spirit and creativity.

Cultivate creativity in the little monkeys? Better to let sharks smell blood. But if it got her Teacher of the Year, she'd suffer through it like a seasoned soldier. She studied the masks one by one. One girl had glued yellow yarn and braided it into pigtails. Others had brushed on lips and cheeks with rosy-pink paint. Several had applied papier-mâché over the eyeholes and had painted the eyes blue, black, or brown.

Her inspection traveled to Christopher's mask. She froze, shot to her feet, and stalked over to his project, her face gone hot from neck to hair roots.

"It can't be."

But it was. Gaping sockets, slanted in a V, as sinister as when she had chastised him. But how? When she'd locked up yesterday, they had been filled in. Otherwise, she wouldn't have let him leave. He must have broken in somehow, but a glance at the windows showed they were locked from the inside. Did he pick the door lock? That seemed unlikely. Christopher was dirty and disheveled, obviously poor, but he didn't have the streetwise swagger of a ghetto brat trained to break into cars.

She examined the eyeholes. The papier-mâché had not been torn away. She doubted that even a sharp knife could have sliced through the hard layers so neatly. And a drill would have left frayed edges, not these smooth openings.

He'd been determined to make the mask *his* way. This wasn't the Spanish Inquisition, but she had her methods to extract information, and extract it she would.

She was on him the moment he was seated, standing before him with the offending object.

She tapped near the eyeholes. "Explain this."

Unblinking eyes stared up at her. "It wants to look that way."

"Not in my class." She gave him a bowl of water, scissors, and a roll of prepared papier-mâché.

"Fill them in, and then you can sit there," she said, pointing to the punishment chair across the room, "until you tell me how those eyes reopened."

When he had laid down strips up to the border of human eye sockets, she marched him to the chair. "Well, are you ready to confess?"

He gazed up at her, the picture of innocence. "It goes that way."

"Fine. Keep both sides of your bottom there, or I'll glue it down with this." She held up a tube of Super Glue and gave it a little shake. Then she leaned close enough to his face that she smelled her own breath—festering Jenny Craig Sunshine Sandwich mingled with stale coffee and non-dairy creamer. "Do you know what happens if this glue seeps through your pants?"

His hair flopped as he shook his head.

"It cements. We'll have to tear your skin to release you. You won't like that, will you, Christopher?"

He shook his head again, his beetle eyes bulging. She walked away, leaving him to ponder the image of ripping flesh. The point here was intimidation and control. She'd never actually applied Super Glue. Never had to. And nail polish remover dissolves the adhesive. But the little cretins didn't know that.

Word problems and spelling took them to recess. First-draft reports on *Jason and the Argonauts* took them to lunch. Christopher wriggled like any nine-year-old but kept both cheeks planted on the chair. And refused to confess.

"Well?" she asked, at the end of the day.

"The mask," he replied in a hoarse whisper. "That's the way *it* wanted it."

She stabbed the air by his face with a finger. "Your artistic vision doesn't matter. In my class, you do what I say. Is that clear?"

After he left, she drummed her fingers on her desk and eyed the mask.

Don't let him get to you, Jessica.

But he was. The little gremlin had stonewalled her. A blatant act of defiance. But a more serious problem needled her. How had he changed the mask? If he could do it once, he could do it again. Disruptions to her plans would not be tolerated, not with the board's visit just days away. The solution was clear. Take the mask home. That would keep it from prankish little fingers.

That night, she skipped the bath, skipped the chardonnay, and mixed herself a stiff Manhattan. She savored another glass after dinner while watching reruns of *Sex and the City*, and then was ready for a blissful night sinking into 100 percent microfiber, 1500 thread-count sateen sheets. She was out like a light until the cocktails began to wear off and dreams intruded. The first were wish fulfillments: a Caribbean cruise, a moonlit beach, a walk with a handsome stranger dressed in white silk. Farther into the night, her dreams darkened. She was sleeping in her bed and thought she heard that primitive drumming.

It's just a dream, she thought, still dreaming. *Just drips from the bathroom faucet. Better call the plumber.*

Or maybe it was raindrops, falling on the windowsill. But the drumming came from downstairs.

From the basement.

It grew louder, as though a whole village was beating, savage and feral. Small figures crept into her room. At first she thought they were pygmies. The females were dressed in grass skirts embellished with beads. The males wore loincloths made from animal skins. Cow-tail tufts covered their upper arms and calves, lending bulk to stunted limbs. In the shadows, their heads seemed huge, misshapen, monstrous. As they stepped into the narrow band of moonlight slanting past her curtain and surrounded her bed, she saw that they wore masks. Fanning feathers adorned the crowns. White straw hanging down the sides framed black, gray, and red geometric patterns painted on the front.

But what arrested her attention, what sent her nervous system into overdrive, were the large, slanted eyeholes.

Like Christopher's mask.

They danced, stepping to the beat of the drums. They stuck small wooden flutes through the mouth holes. A moment later, shrill almost deafening whistling pierced her ears, as if sprites or furies swarmed the room. She tried to shout, No! Paralysis gripped her mouth, as though something had been clamped over it, and she could only make sounds like a stroke victim.

One of the pygmies stepped near. His mask was larger and had been painted several shades of dark brown. He danced closer, leaned over, and peered down at her. For the first time, she noticed that below the skirts, loincloths, and cows tails, the flesh was pink. They weren't pygmies. They were children. Children from her class.

They crowded in. The one with the brown mask—it had to be Christopher—jumped on her bed. He stamped and flailed from one end of the bed to the other. The mattress bounced until her stomach roiled with nausea. The drum beat faster, louder. The flutes screeched, and she drove her fingers into her ears. Christopher sprang and landed with a foot on each side of her. He bent, bringing the ugly brown mask close, so she was face to face with the black lidless eyes, like two yawning abysses. She tried to scream, and fright jarred her awake. Her eyes flared open. The mask lingered, superimposed over her moonlit ceiling, and then melted away.

Drenched in sweat, heart racing, she fumbled in her night-table drawer for a pack of Winstons and a Bic. With trembling hands she lit up and drew in a calming draft of smoke. As she exhaled, she flicked the lighter, watching the flame flare and snuff out. It was a vintage white Bic, purchased to show an aunt that she did not succumb to superstition. Being a left-handed white-Bic owner did not mean she would die like Jimi Hendrix, Janis Joplin, Jim Morrison, and Kurt Cobain. "Be logical, Allison," she'd told her aunt, who was just next door to the mad hatter. "Half the Bics back then were white. It's a coin toss. All chance."

In the dark of night, statistics and probability are fragile things. With Christopher's mask hovering like a phosphorescent phantom in her mind, she crushed out the butt, put on her robe, and went into the kitchen, where she tossed the Bic into the trash. She fished matches from a drawer, lit another cigarette, and made coffee. She drank the pot and chain-smoked, periodically eyeing the paper bag that contained the mask, resisting the impulse to stamp and crush it. When it was time to rise for work, a hot shower restored cold determination. A child would not control her future. She had worked too hard.

She arrived at her classroom early. Today was Thursday and tomorrow was a Teacher Administrative Day. Jessica had sounded out Mr. Jeffries about skipping the mandatory training and staff meetings.

"There is a bug going around," he'd said with a wink. "Better take tomorrow off. We wouldn't want you sick next week."

The committee would tour on Monday. Time to display the newly delivered books and the silly posters. If they were impressed with psychobabble and puerile maxims, she could provide the window dressing. She tacked a poster on each of the four walls and suspended a word-mobile from the ceiling. Then she opened a box filled with hallmark classics (*Treasure Island, Tom Sawyer, Pippi Long-stocking, The Secret Garden*) and politically correct volumes (*Roll of Thunder, Hear My Cry; My Abuelita; Sojourner Truth's Step-Stomp Stride*). She laid Langston Hughes's *My People* on her desk and placed the rest in colored baskets at the front of the classroom, above which she pinned a sign: Extra Credit Reading!

The new books would disappear Tuesday along with the posters.

At 8:15 a.m. the children filed into the classroom, sat at their desks, and folded their hands. Christopher entered last. He flopped into his chair and began pulling threads at the edge of a kneehole.

"Christopher!" she said. "Hands folded. Eyes on me."

He complied but continued to slouch.

"And sit up." Voice a little more strident. Phantoms of the night had dissolved. Sun streamed through the windows. This was her dominion. She was back, and the little urchins would know it. Christopher would know it.

How can his mother send him to school like that? Not even a comb through his hair.

She spied rumpled papers sticking out from under the lid of his desk. "What is that?" she asked.

Unblinking eyes gazed back. "Miss?"

"That. That." She marched up to him and pointed at the offending paper. "Open your desk."

He raised the lid and revealed a mass of crumpled homework and class assignments. One of the sheets had chewing gum stuck to it.

"Only here three days and you've cluttered your desk. Clean this up."

"Yes, ma'am."

She handed him a comb from a package she kept for such emergencies. "And do something about that mop." *Or you'll stick out like a sore thumb. All must be neat and tidy on Monday.*

The day was off to a good start. She was in the groove. Nothing would stop her now. She ignored the dark corner in her mind, whispering doubts. But it was that corner that drove her to set the class on a double-long spelling sheet; it was that corner that compelled her to rehearse math calculations with her star students. For if she had done otherwise, she would have had to look in the bag containing the mask, like someone avoiding sidewalk cracks because to step on one broke the devil's dishes. She would not give in. Science and logic were required. And strength. She employed her voice and look with deadly effect. The two lines between her eyebrows, deeper for lack of sleep, were all the more sinister. Little Betsy Becker was sent to the chair. Had she really been too slow to close her book after silent reading? Perhaps a hair. But the real reason was to make an example of her. If the teacher's pet could be punished, then no one was safe.

Confrontation with the bag would soon be inevitable. The mask needed to be completed today so that it was ready for the committee's tour and could be displayed with the others on Monday. After lunch, the children filed in like soldiers on military display, all except Christopher, who had not yet been trained. He wandered by the books and canted his head dreamily at the mobile. She let it slide. There were bigger fish to fry. When he was seated, she placed the bag on his desk and opened it.

Steady, steady, she bade her hands, which threatened to shake, and her heart, which thumped like a—*Don't say it!*—giant drum.

She fixed her gaze on Christopher as she reached into the bag and removed the mask. She wasn't sure what she expected, but it wasn't the little upward curl of his lips. That smile, so unexpected, forced her to look down. What she beheld was impossible. She had taken the mask home, a mask of plain white paper glued over a mold of human features. This was far different. Not only were the demon eyes back—gaping, leering at her—but the mask had been painted so that it looked like dark leathery skin, and ancient, like something unearthed from an archeological dig.

Like the mask Christopher wore in her dream.

She heard a scream, realizing too late that it burst from her mouth, too late to stifle it, and she flung the mask away as if it were a poisonous snake.

For a long moment she trembled, forcing back the desire to sink her fingers into him and shake him by both shoulders. "How are you doing it?" she asked, her voice strangled.

Unblinking eyes stared at her. "I told you. That's the way it wants to be."

In a flash, she dumped papier-mâché materials and tempura-paint jars onto his desk.

"It's disgusting," she said. "Cover it. Cover all of it. And when you're done, you can sit in the punishment chair until you tell me how you're doing it."

Christopher slopped on gluey paper and painted over wet papier-mâché, making a god-awful mess, but it looked like children's art and an attempt at self-portrait, and that's all that mattered. He spent the rest of the afternoon in the chair, holding the tube of Super Glue. While the class worked independently on assignments, she forewent fantasizing about elegant dining at Narcoossee's Grand Floridian restaurant. Instead, she contemplated the surgical removal of slices and strips of Christopher's skin with a dermatome. A colleague who'd undergone skin grafts described the whole process. The site of the donor skin was acutely painful and vulnerable to infection. She found the thought calming. Just the thing for a trying day.

Christopher gave no cause for Super Glue. By day's end, he also hadn't revealed how he'd changed the mask. It hardly mattered. The logical conclusion was sleight of hand. Magicians did it all the time, putting flowers in hats and removing birds. She deposited the mask in the bag and returned home with it, humming. Before-dinner Manhattans lulled remaining doubt. After-dinner cocktails sent her glowing and euphoric to bed, imagining the victory that was hers on Monday.

Alcohol blissfully anesthetized her until early morning,

when she dreamed she was alone in her classroom. Ants emerged from a corner, streamed across the walls and onto the floor. They flowed toward her. She stamped to keep them away. One managed to crawl up her leg. She reached down to squash it with her finger. It changed into a beetle and stared up at her with black unblinking eyes, jolting her awake.

So, the little monster Christopher had wormed into her unconscious. It wasn't magical or sinister. From undergraduate psychology she knew this was nothing more than day residue, those experiences from the day before that found their way into dreams. This was Friday, the beginning of a long relaxing three-day weekend for her. She quickly put thoughts of ants and beetles from her mind. That she'd heard no drums, that no masked dancing children invaded her sleep, confirmed she was in the groove. Victory within grasp, she spent the day shopping for the trip at Nordstrom, Saks Fifth Avenue, and Bloomingdales.

As far as she was concerned, the three-month traveling sabbatical was in the bag. It was simple math: a = stellar recommendations, cultivated with lunch dates and favors; b = student test scores, highest in the state; c = PTA talks and cupcake fundraisers; d = well-behaved class; e = dazzling classroom.

Ergo: $a + b + c + d + e$ = Grand Floridian Resort, here I come!

Of course, the tangible force of her will and absolute dominion over the class was a constant represented by $\alpha\omega$, alpha and omega, for wasn't that who she was to the little brats for six hours and twenty minutes, five days a week, blessed holidays and school vacations excepted?

She finished the day catching a bargain matinee and a meal. At the Olive Garden, she savored the grilled chicken Caesar and a bottle of Perrier. Yes, she'd been rattled, had needed the wine and Manhattans, but whatever doesn't kill you makes you stronger, and she was back. With a vengeance.

A few days' alcohol-generated calories were negligible but must stop. A pudgy figure didn't attract an eighteen-wheel Peterbilt-driving man. Same with cigarettes. Dream Man wouldn't object to smoking, but to maximize her chances of catching him, she needed pearly-white teeth.

These considerations sent her to bed early with thoughts of lounging at a poolside cabana overlooking Seven Seas Lagoon. Her fantasy dissolved into dreams of a blue-eyed stranger right off the cover of a firefighters' calendar, and she awakened refreshed.

But after a hot shower and a cottage cheese and pear breakfast, doubt began to creep in. What if the mask changed while she'd been sleeping? But no, she was stronger than that. She would not give in to fear. The best thing, she thought, was to have a pleasant lunch. And what better person to have it with than Dora Whitman, three classrooms down the hall, an ardent fan of Jessica's, and hardly competition for Teacher of the Year.

They met at a quiet bistro downtown. Dora's hair sprang wild and free from her head in an unabashed Afro. She wore the same kind of loose-fitting skirt and blouse she taught in, a sacrilege to Jessica's way of thinking. A teacher's arrangement of hair and choice of clothing communicated subtle cues to children. Dora's style said, *I'm nurturing, like your mother. You can trust me. Relax and you'll learn.* (Utter nonsense.) Jessica's style said, *We'll have no funny business. Buckle down and learn.*

Jessica would have preferred an inside table, nestled in a corner and far from other diners. But Dora stretched and inhaled deeply. "Let's sit outside," she said. "Don't you just love it when it rains?"

"The forecast is for clear weather through the weekend," Jessica replied.

Dora rotated her shoulder, saying it always swelled before it rained. Jessica gazed skyward and hugged herself from a nippy gust that swept down and fluttered the awning above the entrance. But Dora drew her to one of the curbside tables with a patio heater nearby and a colorful umbrella above. "We'll be cozy here," she said.

Jessica settled into her seat with a sigh. If it weren't the weekend, she could have consoled herself watching high-powered executives striding by in their Brooks Brothers suits when Dora grew tiresome, as she was sure to.

The lunch passed pleasantly enough and was a welcome distraction. Jessica didn't think once about the bag holding Christopher's mask, which sat on a dining room chair at home. For most of the meal, she and Dora skated around the elephant in the room: the selection committee coming day after tomorrow.

Then as the meal was winding up, Dora leaned forward. "You must be excited."

Jessica looked down on her half-eaten lunch—slyly covered with a crumpled napkin—with an expression designed to convey modesty. "I must admit I am."

"Do you think you'll win?"

Of course I'll win, you little fool. "There are so many other fine teachers."

"Not like you! All the good you do will repay you one day. It's karma! Someday I hope a student comes back and tells me how I changed her life. The things we do for them spread from us to them and out into the world like a ripple."

The idiocy of the notion. Jessica could only stare, but certainly her friend took it again as modesty.

"It's the greatest privilege," Dora said. "I hope I become half the teacher you are. Don't you just love it? Being role models, shaping young minds, directing them toward great things?"

At a loss for what to say, Jessica patted Dora's hand. "I'm sure you will. Try a little firmness, dear. I can hear your class from my room."

Dora brought her fingers to her lips. "Oh ..."

Jessica extricated herself with an excuse that she needed to buy shoes, which wasn't far from the truth. She'd purchased some lovely Ferragamos last week, expressly for lounging in the Grand Floridian lobby—the better to keep time when the band struck up ragtime or some good old-time jazz. When they left the restaurant, clouds were closing in, low and dark.

Dora giggled. "So much for the forecast."

Jessica watched Dora until she was lost in a stream of pedestrians. Then she turned and walked in the other direction, crossed the street, and started strolling through a park. But the clouds grew grimmer, and the wind knocked leaves from the trees and sent them whipping and tumbling on the ground.

"Damn Dora's shoulder," she muttered, and headed back home, consoling herself that another teacher believed she would win. And though most of Dora's ideas were childish and as believable as the Easter Bunny, that one was spot on. Yet another part of Jessica bemoaned her spoiled afternoon in town, which diverted her from thoughts of Monday.

And the thing in the bag.

Though as to that, she refused to give in to fear by looking inside. Instead, she microwaved a bag of popcorn and plunked down on the sofa before the TV to watch *Sleepless in Seattle*.

The rest of the day was unremarkable. In fact, one might say it was serene, as was the night. She dropped off to sleep early. Her dreams were sweet and untroubled. And she awakened refreshed. A shadow seemed to have lifted.

When she looked at herself in the mirror the next morning, she smiled with satisfaction. The bags beneath her eyes from those recent troubled and sleepless nights were already fading. Come Monday, she would look the picture of a kindly teacher.

She would set aside her usual Sunday restlessness. (Who

could relax knowing that in a few short hours you were going back to the little monsters?) But set it aside she would, the result of a carefully cultivated, strong, and focused mind. Nothing would deter her from her goals.

She was master.

To prove this she put the dreaded bag on the kitchen table and sat regarding it, her fingers wrapped around a cup of black coffee. She might have convinced herself that she was, indeed, master of her fate, that she was not subject to super-ordinary laws of the universe—to karma—but for a strange magnetic pull to look inside the bag. The mask had changed before. It could again, and then where would she be?

She rose quickly from the table and busied herself with laundry, vacuuming, a thorough cleaning of the bathrooms, and ironing—giving careful attention that the blouse set aside for tomorrow was wrinkle free. But try as she might, she couldn't shake a nagging feeling that something was wrong, something she could only put to rest by looking in the bag. She loaded and ran the dishwasher, she mopped the kitchen floor, she flung open the pages of the novel in the hope that the duke and the pirate would sweep her away to 1816.

The novel wove its magic. The duke was challenging the pirate to a duel, her ladyship's appeals falling on deaf ears—

Drumming broke the spell. A few beats. Then two or three more from above.

A charge of adrenalin shot through Jessica. Her chest tightened. She held her breath. Her gaze darted toward the kitchen where the bag sat, rolled closed. Perhaps she should seal it with electrical tape. But no, that would show weakness, and a splinter of her knew that if she gave in, she was done for.

Then a long drumroll, high beats on tiny drums. She lurched to her feet. Took a step to the kitchen. And exhaled …

It was only rain, pattering on the roof, tapping on the windows. Jessica laughed. After all, forecasting the weather was not an exact science. No algorithm had as yet been discovered that could extract a prediction from the chaos of clouds over the Amazon, the winds whipping across the Pacific, or the currents boiling around the horn of Africa. And how would one calculate the breath from a bird's wing or the swirl of bees in a field of flowering sage?

Rain was rain was rain. It had fallen before Jessica was born. It would fall long after she died. And she, Teacher of the Year, was going to Florida. You could close the book on that.

Mollified, she returned to the Regency era, savoring the carriages and the clothing and how her ladyship was nursing the duel-injured pirate in a barn. Despite his injury, he was pulling her to his hungry lips—

The bang of a drum jolted her from her reverie. For the life of her she couldn't place what it was or where it came from, and then she heard a laugh outside and realized it had been a neighbor's car trunk.

Am I to get no peace? she asked herself. A slow and growing anger gripped her. She marched into the kitchen, ripped open the bag, and took out the mask. No narrow slots greeted her. The eyeholes were human, or as human as she'd gotten out of the boy.

With a sigh she tossed it back into the bag. This time, just to put it out of her mind, she took electrical tape from one of the kitchen drawers, sealed the top of the bag, and carried it downstairs to the basement, where she locked it in a cupboard. To be doubly secure she turned the key on the basement door and slipped both keys into her pocket. There was no window down there. If anyone tried to tamper with the bag, they would have to get the keys. And past her. What child could? What child would try, knowing as a consequence there would be a long hard reckoning.

She returned to the living room, plucked up the book, and searched through the pages, trying to find where she'd left off. The passages seemed unfamiliar, like they came from a different story.

In the distance, she thought she heard an incessant beating. She froze, and the book dropped from her fingers. Drumming drew near. From downstairs? No, outside, just above the pattering rain and coming down the street.

She swore. It was only a car stereo, blasting rap. She told herself to get a grip. Tomorrow she must appear relaxed and confident. She must keep the children in order on the one hand and exude friendliness and warmth toward the committee on the other.

To this end, to lay all doubt aside, she returned to the basement for one more look in the bag. Nothing had changed, though perhaps in the dimness of the single ceiling light bulb the mask appeared somewhat darker. Relieved, she felt certain that all would go well tomorrow. However Christopher had managed to toy with her, he was unable to continue his prank. Perhaps his mother had kept him occupied or out of town for the weekend.

She ate an early dinner, took a hot shower, slipped into bed, and passed quickly into sleep. Her first dreams were pleasant. She walked into the photos from the Disney World brochures, as though they were portals. Waves rolled onto the shore and caressed the sands with a murmur. She strolled with a cabana boy with dark hair and smoldering eyes. They lay down in the moonlight. Tracing his finger down her cheek, he leaned in for a kiss.

Deeper in the night, still with the cabana boy, it seemed she heard the chirping and buzzing of insects. Jungle pressed toward the hotel—lombi trees with their great buttress roots but also limba, iroko, sapele, and ebony trees—encroaching on the road and invading the walkways. From the foliage came the chatter and cries of hyenas, jackals, parrots, and monkeys. Blue and gold feathers flashed through the leaves. Away in the distance rose the beat of many drums, hollowed-log message drums and drums of stretched goat hide. Galvanizing, fiery, they spoke in a language she didn't understand, didn't want to understand. But the meaning vibrated in her bones, and she shivered at the message: gather the tribes, a call to war. And to their enemies: we're coming.

Chanting joined the drums, both getting nearer, and now the jungle had swallowed the roads and walkways and threatened to engulf the front stairs of the hotel. She woke with a start, lips cracked, throat dry, body steamy with sweat. The pounding of the drums still sounded, though remote now, and then faded away.

She gulped down water from a glass on her night table and glanced at the clock. Three a.m. Too late for a sleeping pill. Wake up time was at six. She reached for ear buds and started a guided-relaxation track on her phone. Ten minutes later she drifted into another dream ...

Back with the cabana boy, she pressed against him in a slow dance in one of Orlando's nightclubs, feeling the rhythm of his breath against her cheek. The lights were low, the music sultry. As they circled the polished parquet she glanced at the jazz orchestra. They were composed of children. *Her* children. With a gasp she turned to go, only to find the bartender, the waiters and waitresses, and the maître d' were also from her class.

Impossible. I'm dreaming, she thought, and willed herself to banish the little nuisances. But the floor was now dark earth, the walls and ceiling grew thick with ferns and jungle trees, and the musicians formed a circle around her. They no longer wore tuxedoes but grass skirts and masks. Symbols painted on their skin glowed in the light of a bonfire. They danced. Stamping. Chanting. Gyrating pelvises. Drawing closer. From just beyond the ring came the deafening beat of drums. A diminutive witch doctor passed through the circle—surely it was Christopher, but who could tell? Snakes writhed around his arms and legs, rattling their tails. He wore a great horned mask and held the awful mask, the one she'd wanted changed, in his small fingers. The mask was not just a hideous brown. It was dark and ancient, from the time when fires first flared in the jungle, magic from human hands. He released it, and it floated toward her, lifted on a wind that came from the chanters shaking talismans; from ants streaming down the trunks of the trees; from thousands of black horned beetles swirling inside the circle. Closer came the grinning horror until it was within inches of her face. There it hovered. The incantations stopped. The tribe grew silent, expectant. Then the mask leaped, attaching to her face. Screaming, she clawed at it, seeking to wrench it free.

She pulled and tugged and yanked, and slowly the mask disintegrated like the wings of a dead moth blown apart by a breeze. She found herself tangled in her bedclothes, her heart pounding, the sheet drenched with sweat.

A dream. A hypnopompic hallucination.

But it seemed so real!

Get a grip, Jessica, it was pre-committee-visit jitters. That's been the problem this whole week. Just the mind playing tricks on you. There are no midget witch doctors, voodoo men, or ancient rites for casting spells.

She glanced at the clock: 5:45 a.m. That was good. She had extra time to shower, have a good breakfast, and relax with the morning paper.

Get my head screwed on right.

After a long hot shower, she lingered over a spinach omelet, dry toast, and coffee. With fifteen minutes to spare, she washed and polished three Cortland apples, purchased for today, and put them, wrapped in cheesecloth, in her purse.

She arrived at her classroom early, purse in one hand, the bag with Christopher's mask in the other. The apples were arranged strategically on her desk, as though adoring students had brought her a little gift. After making a circuit of the room—ascertaining that all was in place and unchanged —she straightened the rows of little desks, each a uniform distance from its neighbor. Only when these preparations were complete did she venture a peek at Christopher's mask, telling herself that to look at it sooner was to give in to fear. *That* she would not do. (Though if she were more honest with herself, she would have to admit that the opposite was also true: avoiding the mask might be a sign of terror.) She was in control; she was the master of her fate; she would prove that in a few short hours.

A glance inside quelled any residual doubt. The color was the same smudge of pinks and oranges and whites Christopher had made to cover the ugly brown. She lifted it out and turned it in her hands. The features were the same, a crude attempt at a child's face. To prove once more her mastery over the situation, she brought the mask to her face and looked out at the room. What a narrow, dim view it seemed.

"See? Just paper, flour, and water," she said.

Whistling a little tune in triumph, she strode to the bulletin board and hung the mask above his nameplate. She glanced at the clock. There was still time before the first bell for one more finishing touch. She strolled to the teachers' restroom, scrutinized herself in the mirror, and ran through a mental list. Hair loose but lightly sprayed. Check. Blouse white and wrinkle free. Check. Light application of blush to suggest emotional warmth. Check. Next, she ran through her practiced expressions, touching on the I'll-tolerate-no-nonsense look, but giving special attention to the see-how-kind-caring-and-patient-I-am look. Satisfied that all was in order, she returned to the classroom.

Morning sunlight streamed through the windows. The first buzz of children playing came from the playground. The bustle and commotion gradually grew. A smiling Dora stuck her head through the open doorway and wished her luck. Jessica nodded absently, her mind 2,509.7 miles away in

Orlando. The first bell rang, and the cries and laughter of her class as they came up the corridor broke in on her reverie. With gratification, Jessica noted that as soon as they crossed into her room they became stiff and silent, stepped quickly to their seats, and folded their hands. Even Christopher followed suit rather than loitering at the colorful book baskets or watching the lazy sway of the word-mobile.

"Very good, children," she said. "I see well-behaved ladies and gentlemen, ready to learn." A sprinkling of praise was never unwarranted, especially now when it could bring a proud little smile to normally terrified lips. "Can anyone tell me what today is?"

Emily, bless her brown-nosing little heart, raised her hand. "The visit."

"That's right, Emily. Some very nice people are coming to watch how special you all are. But we're not going to worry about them. We're going to do our spelling, reading, and math as we always do. When they come, we're going to show them our masks. Afterward, if you're really good, we'll have a pizza lunch." She smiled the good smile, practiced just for today. "And we will behave, won't we?"

The singsong reply came as one voice. "Yes—Miss—Lan—sing."

Christopher raised his hand. "And we won't need Super Glue."

A little chill went through Jessica, but she brushed it off. "That's right, because we're going to be on our very best behavior."

The morning ran like clockwork. At 10:15 the door opened, and Mr. Jeffries escorted the committee in—three women and two men. He gave Jessica an encouraging nod. The committee wandered the room, taking in the posters, the word-mobile, the lessons on the whiteboard, and the shiny red apples, while the class continued silent reading. Not one of the little heads glanced up from their books. Who knows if they were really reading? Probably not. But they *appeared* engrossed. That's all that mattered.

The committee stepped to the bulletin board, stopping at each mask, smiling at what they saw until they came to the area of Christopher's nameplate. The broad shoulders of one of the men blocked Jessica's view. She held her breath. Drumming sounded in her ears. She told herself it was just her pulse, the nervousness of the moment. But the sound grew, and her heart would have to be skipping and surging wildly to produce those strange rhythms. Her face vibrated with it, and then it seemed that something fell from her face. Bewildered, she looked to the floor. Staring up at her from the tiles like a ghost was her own face. It lingered a long moment and then dissolved.

The man moved on. That portion of the bulletin board came into view. The room seemed to have grown suddenly hot. There was nothing above Christopher's nameplate but empty space.

Jessica caught her breath and could only gawk. She swung her gaze to Christopher, who stared unblinking up at her. The room whirled. She staggered. Everything seemed to grow dim and narrow, as though seen through slits, and the drumming throbbed and pounded in her ears. In horror, knowing what she would find, she brought her hands to her face. Her fingers struck the hard surface of a mask. But wouldn't the committee have seen it when they walked in? Wouldn't Mr. Jeffries? They were looking at her now, their expressions questioning, and a low wail forced past her lips and rose like a siren until it filled the classroom. She yanked and pulled at the mask. It stuck to her skin. Each tug with her fingers felt like skin was being ripped from her face.

Mr. Jeffries ran to her. "Miss Lansing, what's wrong!"

"Get it off, get it off," she screamed.

He tilted his head, his eyes puzzled. "Get what off?"

"The mask. The bloody mask!" Chanting and the buzz of insects joined the terrible drumming.

"But there nothing—"

"Can't you see what they're doing? Stop them! Stop them!"

He rested a calming hand on her shoulder. She wrenched away, rushed from the classroom, and made a beeline to the staff lavatory, where she clawed at the dark-brown horror grinning back at her in the mirror.

A siren rose in the distance. Five minutes later two paramedics found her twisting and shrieking on the floor, her fingers bloody.

Though she kicked and struggled, she was strapped to a gurney. They wheeled her down the corridor, lined with teachers and students staring dumbly at her, past the selection committee and Mr. Jeffries, who shook his head sadly.

"It's the children," she screamed. "Idiots, can't you see what they're doing?"

Just before she was lifted into the ambulance, Christopher came through the crowd of onlookers.

"Here, Miss Lansing," he said, placing a jar of nail polish remover on her chest. "Maybe this'll help."

The shrieks that followed served one excellent purpose: they drowned out the beating in her ears.

"What's she raving about?" one of the paramedics asked as he and his colleague slid her into the ambulance.

"Something about a mask," the other replied. "Better sedate with two milligrams Lorazapam. This one's on quite a trip."

The man prepared and administered the injection. Just before the drug took her down, Jessica Lansing heard him say, "Too bad. They said she was a good teacher."

AFTERWORD

Wyndano's story in "The Demon Monkeys" had occupied me for some years. I knew he lived in an earlier age, before the events of my novel, *Wyndano's Cloak,* before the shape of lands and seas changed. I knew he wandered far across his world—sitting at the feet of wizards, gleaning all he could of their magic—until he arrived at a lonely mountaintop where he would distill all he'd learned into one powerful creation. There his tale sat in my mind, a cup missing a handle, as Stephen King says. Wyndano couldn't be the hero—I needed Scamp for that. Once I got her, the demon monkeys weren't far behind. Think of the tale as ancient history to *Wyndano's Cloak,* for which you can find a preview ahead.

Many thanks to my wife Sherry for her keen insights and encouragement. I'm indebted to Elle Thornton, Kerry Hall, and Elisa Adler for their helpful suggestions on several stories. Gratitude goes to the Fellowship of Fantasy, who provided writing prompts for three of the tales. Deep appreciation also to my editors, Betsy Beard and Mark Rhynsberger. I always feel a little sad when a project ends, because they're such a joy to work with.

Preview of *Wyndano's Cloak*

by

A. R. Silverberry

Available Now

CHAPTER ONE

The warning whispered in the leaves rustling in a windless dawn. Jen always knew it would come, but the danger had drifted to the back of her mind like a fading nightmare, leaving only a vague clutching beneath the common activities of the day.

She'd been running along the western side of King's Loop, dawn just pushing above the Aedilac Mountains. Silhouettes streaked by, a farmhouse, a barn, a peach orchard heavy with fruit. Her hair streamed behind, catching the wind like a sail. She almost flew, feet barely touching the ground.

Kicking up a cloud of dirt, she veered off the road and cut through a meadow. She spread her arms, feeling the waist-high grass brush her palms as she whizzed by. Leaving the meadow, she ducked into a thicket of trees, dodging low-lying limbs with the thrill of a bird that's found its wings.

She broke into a clearing and headed toward a stream. With a surge she leaped over the water and made for the lone oak near the bank. Here, a ring of rocks collected water in a quiet pool. Only a few hungry skeeter hawks skated across the surface, looking for an early breakfast. Ducks slept in the grass. They raised their heads and started waddling toward her as she untied a leather pouch.

Taking out a handful of breadcrumbs, she flung it to them. They scrambled with straining necks and blaring trumpets. She threw some toward a runt standing uncertainly on the side, but a big white quacker beat him off with a showy rattle of wings.

Jen pretended to slip the food back in her pocket and waited until the others glided into the water. Then she poured the crumbs into her hand and held it out. The runt hesitated, then crept forward until his beak nibbled her palm.

"You're small," she said softly, "but you can be quick. Dart between them."

When the food was gone, she leaned against the tree. King's Loop looked like a ribbon from here, winding through farm and woodland until it met the great gates of Glowan. There it zigzagged through the little town until it came to the Rose Castle, shining like a jewel in the rising sun. The sheer cliff beyond beckoned. She looked away and exhaled, sighing with frustration and longing.

That was when she heard the whispering. Alert, she backed away from the tree and studied it at a crouch. The air was still. The grass motionless. But the leaves stirred and fluttered. Words floated down. At first they were indistinct, as if someone called through a distant snowstorm. One word emerged clearly, and an icy finger traced down her spine.

She heard her name.

She backed away until she squatted on some rocks that extended into the pool. Every muscle—sun-hammered and wind-hardened like metal in a forge—was poised to spring. Phrases whispered down. The only sense she could make was that something was coming. Something dangerous.

She thought of her family. Fear tightened around her heart. She was a hair's-breadth away from running to them. Her feet stayed rooted to the spot. Maybe she'd hear more.

A small splash made her look at the pond. Two more followed, as if someone had thrown pebbles. Nothing had fallen into the water. But ripples spread out and ran into each other. More splashes erupted like tiny volcanoes, until the whole pool was agitated with colliding rings. A circle of calm emerged below Jen's feet, pushing the waves back. Pale and ghostly, a face rose from the muddy bottom of the pool until it floated just below the surface. Little hills and valleys lined the features of an old woman, as if olives lay under the skin.

"Medlara." Jen spoke under her breath, unwilling to believe her friend could hear her.

Medlara smiled, but her expression hardened. Words whispered from the pool. Jen leaned forward, straining to hear. She got little more than fragments, as if a storyteller jumbled the pieces of a tale. One phrase repeated, like a riddle. "If you meet … a harp, you must … If the worst happens, seek the answers—"

Jen dropped to her knees, hoping to catch more. Medlara's hands appeared just below her chin. She clasped them, and lifted her eyes as if she were imploring Jen. She mouthed two words. They might have been, "Forgive me."

Streaks of blue snaked and flowered in the water, as if someone had dropped in dye. Tendrils of mist rose from the surface and licked the ring of rocks. Soon the whole pool was covered. Spilling over the edge, the cloudy vapor surrounded Jen. She backed onto the shore, but the stuff sprouted up on all sides, walling her in, and formed a ceiling above. It crept along the ground until it met her feet. There it paused like an undulating sea.

Jen studied the mist. "She's trying to show me something. But what?"

There was no time to wonder. Fog rose before her like a giant shadow. Black. Forbidding …

She stepped back. Looked behind for an escape route. The fog surged forward and pulled her into the inky darkness.

She could no longer feel the ground, as if everything solid and beautiful that she cared about was being ripped away. She tried to scream but terror rose from the pit of her stomach and froze in her throat.

The rest was a dizzy kaleidoscope of tilting and falling, of wandering lost, with no way out, no way home, no way back to a world of light and love, until the mist melted away and she collapsed, shaking in a pool of sweat.

How long she lay there she couldn't say, but at last she stopped trembling, her heart slowed, and she gulped some big breaths of air and rose. She staggered to the pool. It looked ordinary enough now. A handful of skeeter hawks glided peacefully on the surface.

The morning sun of Aerdem sparkled on the stream. A few birds sang in the tree. Shaking off numb shock, she splashed water on her face, wiped her hands on her breeches, and ran for King's Loop. She streaked through the fields and leaped onto the road, where a few farmers were carting goods to market. Tearing past them, she was vaguely aware they'd stopped to bow to the king's daughter.

WYNDANO'S CLOAK GIFT EDITION

Wyndano's Cloak

Gift Edition

Limited edition hardbacks are only available through the author, at www.arsilverberry.com. Get your signed or unsigned collectible copy now!

Ebook Editions

Ebook editions are available through Amazon, Barnes and Noble, and iTunes.

Wyndano's Cloak

Also from A. R. Silverberry

The Stream

The Fellowship of the Flame, Chronicles of Purpura #1

The Tear of Tybaleth, Chronicles of Purpura #2

ABOUT A. R. SILVERBERRY

A. R. Silverberry writes science fiction and fantasy for children, teens, and adults. His novel, WYNDANO'S CLOAK, won the Gold Medal in the 2011 Benjamin Franklin Awards for Juvenile/Young Adult Fiction; the Gold Medal in the 2010 Readers Favorite Awards for Preteen Fiction; and the Silver Medal in the 2011 Bill Fisher Award for Best First Book, Children's/Young Adult. His second novel, THE STREAM, was honored as a Shelf Unbound Notable Book and was a Fore-Word Reviews Indie Fab Award Finalist in Literary Fiction. He lives in California, where the majestic coastline, trees, and mountains inspire his writing. Follow him at www.arsilverberry.com.

ABOUT TREE TUNNEL PRESS

Tree Tunnel Press publishes fiction and nonfiction books, including *I Love Birds, An Enchanting Coloring Book,* featuring twelve beautiful hand-drawn illustrations of birds. We create products that entertain, encourage, and inspire. Requests for rights or permissions should be directed to: Tree Tunnel Press P.O. Box 733 Capitola, CA 95010

Visit our website, www.treetunnelpress.com, to purchase books and for more information.